THE LEGACY

There was nothing special about the J-Bar ranch in Colorado . . . except that it had thirty thousand acres of prime land and its previous owner had just been murdered, leaving $50,000 in hidden gold. Then the whole territory joined the hunt for the missing fortune; violence and murder became commonplace. But then three heirs arrived from the East — and that is when true chaos erupted . . .

LOGAN WINTERS

THE LEGACY

Complete and Unabridged

LINFORD
Leicester

First published in Great Britain in 2010 by
Robert Hale Limited
London

First Linford Edition
published 2011
by arrangement with
Robert Hale Limited
London

The moral right of the author has been asserted

British Library CIP Data

Winters, Logan.
  The legacy.- -(Linford western library)
  1. Western stories.
  2. Large type books.
  I. Title II. Series
  823.9′2–dc22

ISBN 978–1–4448–0685–4

Published by
F. A. Thorpe (Publishing)
Anstey, Leicestershire

Set by Words & Graphics Ltd.
Anstey, Leicestershire
Printed and bound in Great Britain by
T. J. International Ltd., Padstow, Cornwall

This book is printed on acid-free paper

1

Numbers.

There were a lot of numbers involved in the murder. Ninety-year-old rancher J. Pierce Buchanan shot five times in his bedroom. Three heirs, none of whom lived with the old man. Thirty thousand acres of ranchland. But the number that had everyone's attention was fifty thousand. The missing fifty thousand dollars Buchanan was supposed to have hidden somewhere in or around his Big Springs, Colorado, home. His killer or killers had shot him dead, but there were indications that he had been tortured before his death, leading everyone to believe that J. Pierce's assailants had been trying to pry the location of the money out of him.

J. Pierce had married late in life. His wife, Mae Buchanan had given him three daughters optimistically named

1

Faith, Hope and Charity before life in the hard country had caused her to surrender to its rugged ways; she had died of simple exhaustion. Mae was now buried beneath an elegant stone memorial on the open prairie. J. Pierce could afford such monuments in his later years. Buchanan had wasted much of his early life studying. He had been an artist, an architect, a naturalist in turn, found none of them paid well and moved West to find that ranching on the long plains paid even less. However, simple mathematical laws eventually came into play. That is: if a good heifer can produce two offspring a year and each of these produces two, eventually a man with luck, avoiding the hardest of winters and the worst of the summer droughts, will find himself able to rise in the morning and look out across the long grass prairie and see a virtual sea of red-backed cattle.

It may take fifty years or so, however, as was the case with J. Pierce Buchanan.

In the meantime Faith, Hope and Charity had all chosen to depart for civilized lands and left the old man alone. With no one to spend his fortune on, he hoarded it. After two banks had collapsed under him, J. Pierce took to holding his assets — in gold only, no paper currency was trustworthy in J. Pierce's mind — in a place of safekeeping known only to himself somewhere in the big house itself or on the thirty thousand acres of land he held by the time of his death.

Faith and Charity had never married, but Hope, herself wedding later in life, had conceived two boys and later still, a daughter. Hope apparently had separated from her husband, for the two boys were living in Mississippi while the daughter was somewhere in Ohio. The three had been notified of their grandfather's death.

A reward had been posted for the capture of the killer or killers, but the tenor of the announcements that could be found tacked on trees and fence

posts from Pueblo to Fort Carson seemed to emphasize that locating the fortune in gold was of more importance than punishing the evil doers. This was probably the case.

J. Pierce had been ninety years old. People figured that he had lived long and would probably have passed away of natural causes before long anyway. The gold, on the other hand, was seen to have deathless existence.

There had been only a handful of local citizens on the ranch when J. Pierce was buried without pomp beside his first wife's marble vault on the prairie. Those who had chosen to come were mostly fellow ranchers, local tradesmen who were considering their future with their chief patron gone, and the twenty-three men who worked on the J-Bar ranch.

When these citizens had departed, the prairie held only thousands of grazing cattle too indifferent to mourn. Others would be coming soon enough, and in numbers far exceeding those

present at J. Pierce Buchanan's funeral.

Each of J. Pierce's grandchildren was making his and her way west, seeking their fortunes in a way much different and more effortless than their grand-father had. These were only the tiniest of a fraction of those interested in J. Pierce's gold.

The habitual residents of the ranch — housekeepers, yard men, cowhands — had begun searching for the hidden fortune before grass could sprout over Buchan-an's fresh grave. The house itself, two storeys of log with a pitched green roof, was first to be combed through. Books were thrown to the floor, pantries invaded, rugs torn up, walls thumped and, where suspiciously hollow-sounding, their pan-eling pried free.

On the range, the cowhands, feeling shut out of the carnival, pondered matters and devised plans of their own. The most appealing notion that any of them had come up with was that J. Pierce had hidden the gold in his wife Mae's mausoleum. Why else was that

ten-foot square white marble monument with its carved cherubs located out on the open plains? And so the ranch hands voted to become grave robbers. This sinister plan was thwarted by the ranch foreman and a few loyal men. The ringleaders were fired off the ranch, the others given a scathing sermon on the sanctity of the grave.

Hardly chastened, the remaining cowboys began telling each other stories they recalled of the old man taking long solitary journeys to nowhere, or to Cripple Creek or Castle Rock — anywhere you could name — going and returning unannounced. These tales gave the treasure hunters hope and the men of the J-Bar spent as much time searching for the missing fortune as tending the cattle. Some drifted away and did not return at all. Not that the population on the land shrank with these desertions. Rather, it burgeoned wildly.

Other men drifted onto the J-Bar, inexorably drawn there by the lure of gold that did not have to be dug from

the earth or fought for, but simply discovered. The fringes of the ranch and at times the ranch itself were a magnet for an assortment of drifters, ex-lawmen, soldiers on leave, citizens of Big Springs and environs and flat-out criminals all looking for J. Pierce Buchanan's treasure. A ring of barbed wire had to be strung around J. Pierce's grave and the nearby tomb of Mae Buchanan to keep gold-hunters away from them.

From time to time the various invading groups had run-ins between themselves or with the remaining J-Bar ranch hands who considered the ranch property their own exclusive reserve. There was so much brawling, so much shooting trouble on the J-Bar that the local sheriff Marston Fowler, had taken leave to visit his family down in Tucson, placing the enforcement of local laws in the hands of two indifferent deputies who took the opportunity to do some gold-hunting themselves, leaving the warring factions on and around the J-Bar ranch to their own devices.

Such was the situation when Glen Strange and Bobby Trapp, drifting southward to avoid another brutal Montana winter, rode onto the J-Bar looking for any available work or at least a meal for themselves and feed for their weary horses.

They didn't get off on the right foot. In fact, their welcome bordered on hostile. Emerging from the high-country pines, they held up and paused to look down at the grassy basin below. There were hundreds of cattle visible, but someone had left them on the section for too long. The grass had been sheared off with overgrazing and was yellowing.

'They had better move their cows,' Bobby said, sipping from his canteen. 'That section looks as bad as if sheep had been at it.' That was true. The herd should have been pushed to farther graze. There were two silver ponds visible from where they sat their horses, and to Glen it was obvious that the cattle, left to their own choice, would

prefer to remain near the water, feeding on their habitual pasture despite the fact that it was growing depleted and there was sweet long grass farther down the valley. Cattle could not be allowed to make their own decisions.

'Well, maybe we showed up at the right time,' Glen replied distractedly. His own attention had been divided. Below them, making their way up a switchback trail, three riders were approaching. 'Maybe we can find out from these gents if J-Bar is hiring.'

'Gents' was not the word Bobby Trapp would have chosen. The three riders were sour-faced, ill-dressed, glowering. One of them, they saw as the trio drew nearer, wore a badge on his filthy blue shirt. All three of them were covered with dirt and one of the riders was packing a pick and shovel where his bedroll should have been riding.

'What do you make of them?' Bobby asked his partner, but Glen only shrugged. He was not given to making snap judgments or drawing hasty

conclusions. He sat his gray horse which shifted its feet uneasily as the three riders drew nearer. They could now make out their faces. Two of them had hard, lined cheeks and prominent noses. They might have been brothers. The third, the man with the badge, had a pouty mouth and an unusually large body from the waist down. He spoke to Glen and Bobby before they had even nodded a greeting.

'Turn your ponies around and get off this property.'

'You have a reason for saying that?' Bobby asked, his narrow face flushing across the cheekbones. Bobby Trapp was a fairly small man, but he did not take to being ordered around.

'I have a reason.' The man tapped the badge on his shirt. 'And this gives me the right to move you off the property.'

Bobby had a heated answer ready, but Glen silenced him with a gesture and inquired patiently, 'Is this your property, deputy? Or do you suspect us of some crime?'

'I suspect your intentions,' the deputy said with hostility. His hand lowered a little and settled near his holstered gun.

'Unless you have good cause — ' Glen began. One of the others interrupted.

'You heard Deputy Sheriff Ward! Get off the J-Bar. You're not wanted.'

'Are you the man who does the hiring here?' Bobby asked, speaking through tight lips.

'We ain't hiring,' the cowboy said flatly.

'Sorry to hear that,' Glen said. 'In that case we'll just need water for our horses. Maybe we could cadge a meal.'

'Get lost,' said the man who had not spoken before. All three scowled at Glen and Bobby.

'Nice talking to you, gents,' Glen said, and with a nod at Bobby he heeled his gray forward.

'Didn't you hear me!' the deputy snarled, but Glen just rode past him.

'What did you make of that?' Bobby asked in a low tone after they had

followed the trail around a switchback. Glancing back, he saw that no one had followed them. 'I about expected them to start shooting.'

'I got the same feeling,' Glen said casually. 'But I figure we have a right to go where we wish. There were no signs, no fences and that deputy knew he didn't have the authority to turn us away. What did you want to do, Bobby, apologize to the man and ride back to Montana?'

'You know I don't, Glen, but I doubt this hot temper of mine will ever get us into the kind of trouble your cool disregard can.'

'Cool disregard?' Glen Strange repeated with amusement.

'Whatever you might call it,' Bobby said, removing his hat briefly to mop at his perspiring forehead with his bandana. 'You couldn't have known those three wouldn't open up with their guns once we showed them our backs.'

'No,' Glen agreed, 'but it wouldn't have made a lot of sense for them to do

that, would it? I only wonder what it is that caused them to bother to warn us off in the first place.'

'I couldn't guess,' Bobby Trapp said, 'but I doubt we've found a place to roost. We just water the ponies, see if we can beg a meal and then hit the road again. Wouldn't you agree, Glen?'

'Let's see how it goes,' Glen answered. 'It could be that we've found us a home and don't know it yet.'

They could now make out the big house below them clearly and a row of bunkhouses set farther back in a grove of ancient oak trees. Outbuildings were scattered here and there, what seemed to be a tool shed, and a smith's shop located next to the red two-story barn, the only structure made of sawn lumber.

There seemed to be very little activity in the yard itself and none visible near the cattle herd. However, there was a bustling sort of motion nearby that was quite incomprehensible to Bobby and Glen Strange. Men with shovels were digging at the base of a granite

outcropping up along the flank of a near hill. Four men were marching in a rank across the flats, searching the ground as they went. They passed two men working with pick and shovel at the base of a distinctive twin pine. These barely glanced up at them as they rode past. Both of the working men wore the yellow-striped blue trousers of cavalry soldiers.

'What is all of this, do you think?' Bobby Trapp wondered aloud. Glen only shrugged. Evidently, something was being searched for. Maybe, he thought, one of the cowhands had ridden into camp and spread the news after discovering a pocket of gold ore. He had witnessed a Nevada ranch nearly ruined when all hands pulled out at once to swarm toward a new gold strike.

Now, riding across the flats them-selves, they passed a marble monument ornately carved, with depictions of angels on each corner. It was an oddity on the plains, to be sure, but even

stranger was the fact that it had been surrounded by coils of barbed wire and there were two armed men guarding the monument.

Bobby Trapp muttered, 'Must be a very important cadaver.' Again Glen could only shake his head. The situation was bizarre, disturbing. It was as if they had ridden into a war zone where the troops were either arriving or withdrawing randomly with no one in command of the activity.

'Directly to the main house, I guess,' Glen said, nodding toward the two-story log structure. A guard with his rifle in the crook of his arm had been posted on the front porch, they noticed.

'How about we see to the horses first?' Bobby suggested. 'That way we'll know that they're fed and watered before more people can advise us to move along.'

Glen nodded. It made no difference to him and perhaps Bobby was right. If they were to be run off the J-Bar at least they would have fresher ponies under

them as they continued to drag the line looking for employment elsewhere.

Walking their horses across the yard in front of the main house, they passed only an older man with an ax across his shoulder, a mangy dog skulking after him. There was not much activity for a ranch of this size, that was for sure. Passing through the cool of the shade cast by the spreading oak trees, they came to the red barn. Its double doors stood open and after calling out, both men swung down and led their horses that way.

They were only a few paces from the entrance to the dark barn when a man with a shiny new Winchester stepped out of the shadows, threw his weapon to his shoulder and announced clearly: 'You can get on those mounts and ride off or stand where you are and get shot down.'

2

Both Bobby Trapp and Glen hoisted their hands, reins wrapped around their fingers, but they made no move to mount their horses. The stranger with the rifle took one step forward and sunlight now hit him fully, forming the shadow into a man of middle years, average height and weight with a badly pocked face. The rifle he had positioned at his shoulder did not waiver.

'Both of you hard of hearing, are you?' he demanded.

'Friendly sort of place, isn't it?' Bobby Trapp said in a low voice to Glen.

'Mister,' Glen Strange said carefully, 'I don't know who you think we are, but we're only a pair of drifting cowhands, floated down out of Montana looking for work. Why, in this part of the country, that is a shooting offense

is beyond me. Let us talk to the man who does the hiring around here, won't you, in a civilized way. Then if we're told to go, we'll go — no shooting required.'

'You're talking to the man who does the hiring,' the rifleman replied. 'Turn your pony a little so that I can read his brand, will you?'

Glen shrugged and without lowering his hand, tugged the reins enough so that his gray shifted his position slightly. Burned into the horse's left flank was the Ladder T, a well-known Montana brand, recognized even this far south.

'I suppose you're telling the truth,' the pocked man said, lowering his rifle at last. 'What are you doing here?'

'We heard the J-Bar was along our route. We were told it was a big spread, could possibly use some help, and were told that it was a friendly place where a hungry man could at least cadge a meal,' Glen said coolly.

'Used to be,' the man with the rifle said. 'You sure that's what you boys are

looking for? A meal and maybe a job?' He looked from Strange to Bobby Trapp, his eyes narrowing.

'That's it,' Bobby answered. 'What the hell else would we be looking for? And we noticed that you've a fair-sized bunch of cattle along toward those twin ponds who need to be pushed toward new graze. They've chewed that grass to the yellow nub. We'd be willing to do that job for you — if you haven't got anybody else around here who knows how to get a steer to start walking.'

Bobby was a little sarcastic, but that seemed to go over the rifleman's head. 'We've got plenty of men,' he replied, 'just try and find them.'

Trapp and Glenn exchanged glances. Glen shrugged. 'Mind if we pitch some hay for our ponies?' he asked. 'They've been long on the trail and on poor forage.'

'Go ahead,' the man said, tipping back his hat. 'And get yourself something to eat at the cook shack. Anyone can show you where it is. Maybe I can

use you two — for a while, at least.' He paused, smiled thinly and apologized, 'Sorry for the rough greeting. If you only knew how things have been around here. My name's Ben Case, J-Bar foreman. You boys tend to your horses. I'll be talking to you later about moving that bunch of cattle.'

With their horses seen to, Bobby and Glen Strange crossed beneath the oak trees again, walking toward the first of the bunkhouses they had seen on the yard perimeter. No one else was visible in the area, although once, inexplicably, a trio of horsemen came pounding past them sending up a swirl of dust.

'Wonder where they're going in such a hurry,' Bobby Trapp said.

'No telling. I think we'd better tread lightly for a while, Bobby. There's things going on here that I don't understand.'

'Eyes and ears open, mouth shut?' Bobby replied.

'Exactly that.'

The door stood open at the end of

the log bunkhouse and as they approached it they saw a woman in a blue-checked dress with a white scarf tied over her hair, industriously sweeping. She glanced up at them with hostile eyes and demanded:

'Who are you two supposed to be?'

She was younger than Glen had thought at first. Slender, with slashing dark eyes and a full mouth that seemed ready to spit. She gave the impression of being a gypsy woman or some sort of Spanish mix, but her skin was pale. Glen answered before Bobby could fire back a retort.

'Case told us to come over here and get something to eat.'

'He's going to make that mistake again, is he?' the woman said, leaning on her broom as she gazed through the trees toward the big house.

'What mistake?' Bobby asked innocently.

'Trusting strangers,' she said, biting off her words. The broom was placed aside to lean against the bunk house wall. The woman wiped her forehead

with the back of her hand, sighed and told them: 'Come on in; I can make you sandwiches.'

Inside, they were seated at a long plank table. Beyond this room was a sleeping area, wooden bunkbeds lined up along a rough interior wall. The place was deserted except for the three of them. The woman took a loaf of bread from the breadbox and sawed off four thick slices. From the pantry she took a hanging half-ham and cut it. The sandwiches produced were slapped onto platters and set before Bobby Trapp and Glen, followed by coffee in tin cups poured from the gallon-sized pot on the wood stove.

The woman stood at the end of the table, arms crossed and told them, 'My name is Nora. I don't have a man, don't want one. Stay away from me if you know what's good for you. This isn't my regular work, but the men passing through keep the place filthy and the bunkhouse manager has left. He got sick with the gold fever like everyone

else in this part of the country.

'I'm telling you this so you'll know — if you want to eat, feed yourselves. If you want to live in a clean place, clean up after yourselves. Don't call for Nora, because Nora won't come to the aid of grown men who should know how to take care of themselves.'

With that, she gave a little nod, stepped outside and off the steps to move through the mottled sunlight beneath the oaks, striding toward the big house.

'That was friendly,' Bobby said around a mouthful. Glen shrugged.

'She was only telling us the way things were before we got other thoughts.'

'Yes, but there are other ways of saying things,' Bobby said. After a minute, he swallowed a bite of food and asked, 'Did you hear what she said about gold fever, Glen? Do you figure we were right and someone found a little vein of it or maybe a few nuggets in a creek?'

'Seems like it,' Glen answered, although the way men were running around the yard and the surrounding hills, they little resembled would-be gold miners. 'Someone will tell us, I suppose.'

The someone was a little white-haired man with red cheeks and sunken eyes who made his way into the room as Glen and Bobby were finishing their coffee. He blinked at the two of them and came ahead, carrying a load of kindling in his arms. This he stacked near the iron stove.

'Where's Nora?' the old man asked, dusting sawdust from the sleeves of his faded red shirt.

'She left,' Glen said. 'I suppose she had more important things to do.' He then introduced himself and Bobby Trapp. The old man shook hands with both of them.

'You can call me Tiny,' the old man said with a smile that showed only a few remaining teeth. He rubbed his spindly arms and shook his head. Leaning

against the kitchen counter he told them, 'They always called me Tiny, you see? For years I was the fattest tub of lard you'd ever seen astraddle a cow pony. Then I got sick — real sick. When I was well I found that I had lost a few pounds, which was natural. Then I discovered that I was getting old, boys, and that my appetite was simply gone. Now they call me Tiny,' he mused, 'and I am!'

Glen said nothing. The old man apparently enjoyed telling the story. Bobby, brash as ever, wanted to know: 'What's this we hear about gold fever, Tiny?'

'That?' Tiny frowned, poured himself a cup of tepid coffee and answered. 'You mean you made it all the way to the ranch without seeing the signs they tacked up? Maybe someone's been tearing them down, now that I think of it, not wanting competition.'

'There was really a gold strike?' Bobby said, interested now.

'No, sir,' Tiny said, scowling. 'Here's

what happened.' And he proceeded to tell them the story of J. Pierce Buchanan and his missing treasure. Tony said that J. Pierce's three grandchildren were on their way West and that the gold hunters seemed to be determined to find Buchanan's gold before his heirs arrived.

'Don't his banker know where the money is?' Bobby asked. 'Or his lawyer — there must be a lawyer.'

'Old J. Pierce didn't like banks. He didn't like lawyers either, but he had one. A man named Dumont, but after notifying the heirs, he can't do much until they arrive for the reading of the will.

'So meanwhile,' Tiny went on, 'we've got everybody and his brother out looking for the gold. Men I never saw before who come here with nothing but a shovel. We've got some army deserters, men from the neighboring ranches and most of our own crew out there digging up the ground wherever they take a notion that it might be hidden.

First thing torn up was the big house, of course. Household staff and some of the hands took care of that. Ben Case ran most of them off. He's foreman and he can't do anything but watch as the ranch goes to hell. Old man Buchanan took him in when Ben was on the run — so I hear — rehabilitated him and trusted him enough to make him foreman.'

'A former outlaw, is he?' Bobby asked.

'It's been rumored, but no one knows any of the particulars. I only know that Ben Case was fiercely loyal to Buchanan and to the J-Bar brand. Him and Nora.'

'Why Nora especially?' Bobby asked. Glen was only listening. He rose and touched the coffee pot with his fingertips. It was nearly cold but he poured himself another cup anyway.

'You wouldn't believe it, but she was abandoned by her folks. Right here on this ranch. A regular foundling. Buchanan's daughters were long gone by

then, and he took to Nora right away. Took her in and brought her up.'

'She's not an heir?' Glen asked, interrupting for the first time.

'Not that anybody knows. You might notice that Nora has an edge on her. She was never that way with the old man, but she can be sharp with most everyone else. Buchanan raised her that way. Said she wouldn't be brought up genteel like he had done with his daughters. Said that spoiled a woman.'

'Who's working the ranch now?' Bobby wanted to know.

'Well,' Tiny said with a frown, 'you two boys, if you mean to stick, and the three Fain brothers. They're over on the south range just now. They're loyal. A couple of others too old or lazy to be greedy. Most of the other boys are gone. They drift in after a few days of gold-hunting expecting to find their bunks still waiting for them, but Ben Case, he told me when that happens, just to roll up a man's mattress and throw his gear in the barn, because

that man ain't working for J-Bar any-more.'

'We saw a couple of men guarding that monument, whatever it is,' Bobby said.

'That was Buster Haynes and Len Crutcher. Len can't walk too well and old Buster can hardly see. They're about useless, but J. Pierce never had the heart to cut them loose. Who knows what will happen to them now. The monument you're talking about, that is Mae Buchanan's grave. Once the jackals got it in their heads that there was gold to be found, they decided that it was a likely hiding place.'

'Can't the law do something about this?' Glen asked. 'People are trespassing, destroying private property.'

'The law has joined them,' Tiny said sorrowfully. 'What we have of it, that is. Sheriff Fowler went to Arizona. All we got is his two no-good deputies.'

'We saw one of them, Glen, remember?' Bobby Trap said. 'Riding with two soldiers.'

'That would be Abel Ward,' Tiny said. 'He's greedy and weasel-smart. The other deputy's name is Po Hilgers. He's greedier yet and weasel-stupid.'

'Think they'd shoot a man?' Bobby asked, glancing at Glen.

'Would they? I don't know,' Tiny said. 'Who'd stop them?'

There wasn't much Bobby and Glen could do that afternoon with the sun heeling over toward the western mountains and their horses resting, so they offered to split some firewood for Tiny who was more than willing to show them the woodpile.

By evening, between the two of them they had split nearly half a cord of wood. Looking to the darkening skies, Glen halted, placed his ax aside and mopped the sweat from his forehead.

'Tiny said to take half of this wood up to the big house,' he told Bobby. 'If we're going to do that before dark, we'd better start.'

Bobby Trap glanced toward the sky too. The light through the huge oak

trees was a deep purple. The day which had been warm was rapidly cooling. He nodded, placed his own ax aside and began loading split logs into the four-wheeled barrow at hand. With Glen doing the pulling and Bobby the pushing they made their way up the winding path to the main house. There was no guard now on the porch; a lantern hanging on an iron hook burned low, illuminating the front of the log building.

'Wonder where they want this — ' Bobby began, but he was interrupted by the near explosion of a rifle shot.

'Inside the house,' Glen said, dropping the wheelbarrow handle, pawing his Colt from its holster. The two rushed to the front door, shouldered it open and entered to find Nora, Winchester in her hands, standing in the middle of the living room. Her dark hair was down, her eyes set. They flashed with excitement as she glanced at them and started to bring the muzzle of her rifle around

before she recognized them.

'Outside the window,' she said, slowly lowering the weapon. Looking that way, Glen saw that a large pane of glass had been shot out. He walked that way, the acrid scent of gunpowder still heavy in the air.

'Who was he?' Bobby Trapp asked.

'Another prowler,' Nora replied. 'They'll take any opportunity to get in and search the house,' she waved a hand around the disordered room, 'even though it's been combed through and torn to a shambles already.'

'You got him,' Glen said, leaning out the window.

'Of course I did,' Nora said sharply. 'Get him out of here. Plant him somewhere.' She paused and then asked, 'What are you two doing up here, anyway?'

'Tiny told us to bring you some firewood,' Bobby Trapp answered. He had wandered up beside Glen to look out the window at the heavy-set dead man who lay crumpled against the earth.

'Who was he?' Bobby asked.

'He didn't introduce himself,' Nora replied coldly. 'You boys remember that — use the door and knock before you enter.'

They would remember that, certainly. After bringing in several armloads of wood for kitchen use, they hauled the rest of the split logs around to the wood shed behind the house. Unloading it, Bobby commented, 'Glen, if this isn't the damndest place!'

'It is,' Glen agreed, glancing up from his work shifting logs. 'I think we should maybe just stay around long enough to make sure our horses are fat and rested and we've got a little silver to chink in our pockets as we ride.'

He got no argument from Bobby. The J-Bar smelled of trouble. The ghost of J. Pierce Buchanan might have departed the scene, but the lost gold continued to haunt the ranch.

Digging a grave for the dead man at a decent interval from the house, they were approached by an anxious-looking

red-headed man riding a pinto horse. Seeing them digging, the stranger reined in his horse, leaned down and asked excitedly:

'Found something?'

Glen only nodded at the dead man lying nearby and the disappointed gold hunter rode away into the darkness.

'The place has a sickness about it,' Bobby grumbled after the stranger had gone on his way. 'Plague, is more like it.'

Glen paused, leaning on his shovel. Looking at Bobby Trapp, he asked his partner, 'What would you do with fifty thousand dollars, Bobby?'

'Me? Put it to practical use,' Bobby Trapp answered with a smile. 'Find me a young widow and hand it all over to save us both the time and trouble of her tricking me out of it.'

Glen chuckled and they returned to filling in the grave of the unknown man. He told Bobby, 'Me, I figure they're all wasting their time. Once the heirs arrive and the lawyer reads the will, it'll

probably be made clear where the gold has gotten to. I didn't know Buchanan, but I judge he was no fool, not fool enough to lose that much money.'

It had been a long day, and after returning the barrow and placing their axes back in the tool shed, both men were ready for a bite to eat and a bunkhouse cot.

Night settled slowly and gently. After a meal of beef and potatoes, the two decided to turn in early. They had ridden far and the afternoon's labor had done nothing to ease their weariness. They grabbed their blankets and spread them on two adjacent empty cots. Outside the bunkhouse the only sound was that of the oak trees shifting slightly in the wind. In the bunkhouse there was the soft glow of the stove fire still burning in the kitchen. Glen Strange tugged off his boots and lay back staring at the rough ceiling, hands behind his head. He was nearly asleep when the sound of Tiny's approaching footsteps caused

him to briefly lift his eyelids.

'How do you like J-Bar after your first day?' Tiny asked them, sitting on a bunk nearby.

'Half a day,' Bobby Trapp corrected, 'and it strikes me as the strangest spread we've ever been associated with.'

Tiny smiled and shook his head. 'I suppose it is — now. J-Bar used to be a proud brand. Men rode in from all over wanting to sign on. It's all different now, with the old man being dead.'

'That troubles me,' Bobby said, sitting up in his bed. 'I haven't heard a word about anyone trying to find out who murdered J. Pierce. All the talk's been only about the missing fifty thousand. Doesn't anyone care what happened to Buchanan?'

'I suppose people are mostly worried about themselves, like people anywhere,' Tiny considered. 'They probably figure it's the law's business and none of their own to find the killer.'

'Buchanan wasn't well-liked, then?'

Glen Strange asked from behind closed eyes.

'He was liked well enough,' Tiny said defensively. 'I suppose he had gotten a little crotchety of late. They tell me that that's not uncommon in persons above a certain age. I have to admit to being a little that way myself.'

'Still, you'd think people who cared for the old man would be wanting to find out what happened to him. What about Ben Case and Nora? You said they were both more or less rescued from the wild world by J. Pierce. Nora a foundling, Ben Case a man on the run.'

'I can't speak for them,' Tiny said uneasily.

Glen Strange rolled onto his side and spoke again, his eyes fixed on Tiny. 'Is there something between the two of them? Nora and Ben Case, I mean?'

'I wouldn't know about anything like that,' Tiny said stiffly. 'Why would you ask?'

'I don't know,' Glen said. 'Maybe Nora knew she wasn't mentioned in

Buchanan's will and resented it after living as his daughter for all these years. Maybe she told Ben Case that. Maybe she mentioned the fact that with J. Pierce gone, the ranch would fall to the foreman for its management.'

'Who says she's not in the will!' Tiny said, obviously offended by Glen's speculation. 'No one's seen it. Maybe she is. Maybe both of them.'

'All the more reason to wish J. Pierce out of the way,' Bobby Trapp couldn't help putting in. 'Some people aren't willing to wait for what they think they have a right to.'

'It could be that Nora found the hidden gold before anyone else even knew Buchanan was dead,' Glen said for the sake of discussion. 'No one knew Buchanan's ways and that house's hiding places better than she would.'

'I don't think I wish to be talking to you two men anymore,' Tiny said rising to his feet. The thin, white-haired man was obviously

incensed. The idea that two strangers could ride in here and practically accuse Buchanan's adopted daughter and the ranch foreman of plotting to murder the old man was repugnant to him.

'Sorry,' Glen Strange said, seeing how upset the old man was. 'We were just considering matters. Maybe no one else around here is interested enough to try to find those responsible for killing J. Pierce, but I am.'

'*You* are!' Tiny sputtered. 'Why would you care?'

'I dunno,' Glen said, shutting his eyes again. 'Buchanan being gunned down like that — it sort of offends my sense of propriety. Besides, if my luck holds, I have intentions of becoming an old man myself one day.'

After Tiny had stamped away in indignation, Bobby Trapp said, 'You sort of rubbed his fur the wrong way, Glen. Why did you start that?'

'Why? I don't know. I'm usually pretty good at keeping my thoughts to

myself, but something about the situation bothers me, Bobby. And, don't forget, whatever's going on, we're smack in the middle of it now.'

3

Two of the Fain brothers, young, blond and cocky, arrived in the morning to help Glen Strange and Bobby start the cattle gathered near the twin ponds toward better graze to the south. The cows were balky but not indignant. It was a short drive and an easy one with only a few of the steers making a break for it. The Fain brothers, Rod and Austin, rode well-trained, energetic cutting horses and they had no trouble drifting these back toward the herd. Glen was aboard a placid black mare whose idea of driving cattle seemed to be to bump into their flanks with her shoulder. His gray needed another day's rest, but he was missing the sturdy little animal already.

At noon the four men stopped on a grassy knoll to eat salt biscuits and bacon Rod Fain sliced and fried. Austin

was by far the more talkative of the two blond J-Bar riders, and he sat beside Glen, filling in some of the gaps in his knowledge of the events on the ranch. Fain's conclusions were dismal for his own and the J-Bar's prospects.

'Those children of J. Pierce, that girl and the two boys, they won't want to take over the ranch. Like as not they'll have the lawyer try to sell the place off.'

'Leaving Ben Case ranch manager?' Glen asked as the two sat cross-legged on the grass, eating.

'Who else? Of course that leaves us all in an uncertain position,' Austin said. His brother approached them with an iron pan filled with frying bacon. Glen Strange was watching the cattle who had now settled on their new graze, a few of them lined up along the small silver-blue creek that wound through the willow trees in the valley.

'There's a lot of money on the hoof out there,' Glen said, 'and from what you tell me, twice that many on the south range. There's a profit to be had

for anyone wishing to sell them.'

'And who'd drive them to market?' Austin asked dryly. He leaned back on his elbows, squinting into the afternoon sun. 'We've no hands who are willing to work cattle anymore. Everyone is out looking for quick money. Buchanan's gold.'

'Did that ever actually exist?' Glen Strange asked. 'I mean, did anyone ever see it, or is it just one of those stories that grow up around a dead man.'

'Oh, old J. Pierce had it, all right,' Austin Fain said confidently. 'The money I've seen him make off his herds — it was big money, Glen. And, it's true that J. Pierce never trusted banks. So where did he put it? Hell if I know, but he certainly did have fifty thousand at a minimum.'

'Hell of a lot of money,' Glen commented.

'It is, taken all at once. But look at it this way, Glen, J. Pierce worked this range since he was forty. That's fifty years of work. He had no expenses.

Me,' Fain said with a grin, 'if I could work for a dollar a day for the next 136 years with no outgo, I'd have fifty thousand, too.'

'And that's just your average cow-hand!' Glen Strange said, smiling as he rose to dust off the bottom of his jeans.

'Yeah, well, J. Pierce made a hell of a lot more than a dollar a day, and my point is that over fifty years he could easily have had that much tucked away.'

'I was thinking — you don't suppose someone's already found the money?'

'I thought of that,' Austin said. 'If it was me who found it, I'd be long gone by now. But someone smarter might hang around just to watch the show until the uproar had settled.'

'Nora?' Glen Strange suggested, and Austin Fain's affable smiled faded. He answered tightly:

'Don't say a word about Nora.'

Glen shrugged an apology and watched as Austin Fain trudged away toward the campfire where he helped his brother kick out the flames and

repack the eating utensils. Glen Strange watched silently and then started that way. Well, well, Nora seemed to have a full complement of protectors. Tiny, Ben Case, Austin Fain — all of them seemed very loyal to the dark-eyed woman. They knew her better than he did, of course, but she was hardly a charmer and Glen Strange wondered what sort of hold the woman had on them all.

Reaching the dead campfire, he saw the two Fain brothers staring south-ward across the long valley. Rod Fain lifted a pointing finger and his brother nodded.

'What is it?' Bobby Trapp asked.

'Train must have arrived. Here they come.'

'Who?'

'Unless I miss my guess, that landau and team of matched bays belongs to Craig Dumont. There's a woman sitting beside him and two men riding in their dust. It looks like the heirs apparent have found their way to the J-Bar.'

Glen stood watching as the buggy neared. Fain had been correct about a woman being among them. He could see nothing of her face, but he saw a few strands of blond hair flying free from her blue bonnet. She was in a blue dress with black trim. No veil. Of the two men Glen could tell even less except that each wore tan suits cut for town living. Only one of them wore a hat, a white planter's style topper with wide brim.

'We'd better get to work, boys,' Rod Fain said with a smile. 'They see us loafing we might get ourselves fired.'

Austin managed to laugh at his brother's joke. Glen Strange and Bobby Trapp only exchanged a glance. They had just begun to put down roots; neither was ready to travel on just yet.

They all mounted and rode at an angle down the long hill, veering away from the approaching party.

'Don't you want to introduce yourselves?' Bobby Trapp asked the Fain brothers. 'Take a closer look at them?'

'I'll be happy if I never have to get closer to any of them than I am right now,' Austin Fain replied, and he meant it. Both of the Fain brothers seemed to be harboring some resentment beyond those of the general circumstances. For himself, Glen Strange thought, he wouldn't mind taking a closer look at J. Pierce's grandchildren. After all, one of them might be their future employer.

And, he thought, he wouldn't mind taking a closer look at the blond girl who rode, back erect, on the bench seat beside the lawyer.

Austin was saying, 'You two boys might as well head back and see what Ben Case wants you to do next. Rod and I are going to go on to the south range and see if our brother needs any help.'

With that, the Fain brothers started their horses away and with a last glance at the new arrivals, Glen Strange and Bobby began riding back toward the main ranch. They didn't get far.

There was a shout from the road

below and then another. As Glen turned in the saddle he saw two mounted men burst from the willow brush along the creek and ride toward the landau, guns drawn.

Neither Glen nor Bobby Trapp spoke. They wheeled their ponies and started down the grassy hill toward the confusion on the trail. One of the attacking men had grabbed the bridle of the lead horse while the second swung his pony up beside the carriage on Craig Dumont's side. The two men who had been riding with the carriage, the Buchanan brothers, stuck spurs to their mounts and fled in the direction of the Buchanan house.

When Glen was within pistol range he saw one of the attacking riders look up and shout a warning, pointing a finger at him. Bobby Trapp fired his weapon at one of the raiders, but the shot went wild. No matter, the shot served its purpose. The attackers heeled their horses roughly away from the besieged wagon. Bobby was in pursuit

before Glen could stop him. The two ambushers were now far ahead, but Bobby continued to flag his sorrel horse with the ends of his reins, trying to run them down. Glen reined in beside the landau. The blond girl rose to her feet in the wagon box and peered northward where her brothers had long vanished.

'So much for family loyalty,' she muttered.

'Are you all right,' Glen asked, including Craig Dumont in his glance although he had eyes mostly for the pretty slender girl beside him.

'Yes,' Dumont said.

'The two men who were chased off — ' Glen started to inquire.

'Cowards,' the girl snapped. She was still glaring in that direction. Now her blue eyes shifted to Glen Strange and her mouth softened. She seated herself, smoothing her blue skirt.

'I'm Amanda Buchanan,' the woman said. 'This is Mr Craig Dumont, our family attorney. Those rats who just ran away are Earl and Charles Buchanan.

My brothers,' she added bitterly.

'Glad to meet you. My name's Glen Strange,' Glen said, touching his hat brim.

'Do you work for the J-Bar?' Dumont asked. He was a narrow man with a spider scar on his cheek as if he had been shot in the face at some time. His eyes were unlighted slate gray behind gold-framed spectacles.

'This is my second day,' Glen said with a grin. 'It's been an experience.'

'I can imagine,' the lawyer said. 'Do you mind if we continue on our way? We can talk while we ride.'

'Please stay with us,' Amanda Buchanan said, and there was no refusing those blue eyes. 'Those men who attacked us might come back.'

'Who were they?' Dumont wanted to know. He snapped the reins to start the frightened horses forward once more. 'And why assault us?'

'I've seen them before,' Glen said. The two riders with their sharp cheekbones and prominent noses were

the same he and Bobby had encountered the day before riding with Deputy Sheriff Ward. 'They're a couple of the fortune hunters. As to why they stopped you, I'd guess they figured there was a chance that as Buchanan's lawyer you might have a strongbox full of gold with you.'

'What gold?' Amanda asked with blank curiosity.

'I'll explain it all at the reading of the will,' Dumont told her. 'Somehow word has gotten around that your grandfather stashed a fortune in gold somewhere on the J-Bar and searchers have arrived like swarming locusts, from what they tell me.'

Glen nodded agreement. His black horse had fallen into step with the landau's team. Amanda continued to chat easily. The sun flickered through the willows and from time to time they could see the silver-bright sheen of the creek flowing through the trees.

'Where did your friend go?' Amanda asked Glen Strange.

'Bobby? He'll chase those two for awhile until he or his horse gets tired of the game. I doubt there'll be any more shooting. Those men didn't seem anxious for a fight.'

'Nor did my brothers!' Amanda said, her irritation returning. 'I always imagined that I had two big brave brothers living down in Mississippi. You know, mother and I lived in Ohio — I still do — mother's dead now. So when we exchanged letters and an occasional gift I would miss my brothers although they are twenty years older than I. What a disappointment!'

'Life's full of them,' was Glen's only comment. He didn't know the Buchanan brothers. Maybe surprised, perhaps unarmed, they had seen their only option as taking flight. Every man is not a born fighter. Glen, for example, doubted he himself would have ridden off in wild pursuit of the bad men as Bobby Trapp had. Glen Strange spent a lot of time trying to avoid trouble himself. As he had told Tiny, he had

hopes of one day being an old man. He didn't intend to finish out his time on earth aimlessly like one of those drunken kid gunfighters gunned down in his prime.

'How far is it to the house?' Amanda asked, fanning herself with her hand.

'Only about a mile,' Dumont answered.

Bobby Trapp was riding toward them, his pony flecked with sweat. He wore a big grin, and approaching Glen, he said, 'I couldn't catch them, but I tried.'

'They'll think twice next time,' Glen said.

'Maybe. It seems some folks never learn, though.'

Introductions were made and they continued on toward the big house, following the road which now wandered away from the river.

Amanda asked Bobby, 'Did you see my brothers anywhere?'

'Those two men riding with you? Is that who they were?' Bobby said. 'Yes, they were just tying up in front of the

house when I passed.'

The Buchanan house was now coming into view. Amanda made a small, indefinable noise with her pursed lips as she studied the imposing log structure standing among the ancient oak trees.

'This the first time you've seen the place?' Glen asked.

'Yes. I've never even been West before. It's not the sort of house you see in the East, but it looks . . . substantial.'

'The inside might be kind of a disappointment to you,' Glen had to tell her. 'There have been burglars, gold hunters in there, tearing things up.'

On the porch now they could see Nora, hands on hips, her dark eyes watching their approach. Just stepping up onto the front porch was Ben Case. Behind Nora in the doorway Earl and Charles Buchanan also watched their arrival.

'Good,' Craig Dumont said, 'everyone is here.'

'Who are they?' Amanda asked in a near-whisper, indicating Nora and Ben Case, and Dumont gave her a brief explanation.

'But they're certainly not mentioned in the will!' Amanda exclaimed. Dumont gave her no answer. Apparently he was not going to reveal anything about the terms of the will until it was time.

Now was obviously not the time to ask Ben Case what he wanted Glen and Bobby to do in the way of work for the rest of the day, and so Bobby leaned over and said to Glen. 'Let's take these nags over to the barn and saddle our own ponies.' Glen nodded agreement, but Amanda had overheard and she spoke up with some urgency.

'Glen! I want you to come along with me.' She said this almost as if she expected foul play in the house once the provisions of the will were read. He smiled and stuttered an answer.

'I hardly think that — '

'I mean it,' she said resolutely and she fixed pleading eyes on him. Glen

glanced questioningly at Craig Dumont who only shrugged as if to say, 'Why not, if it makes her feel better?'

Glen swung down from his horse, nodded goodbye to a puzzled Bobby and helped Amanda down from the buggy. She smiled her thanks, then glanced at the house and scowled. Apparently the episode on the road had soured her on trusting her long-lost brothers. At any rate, she doubtfully started up the steps to the porch holding her skirts high. Nora eased aside, unsmiling herself. Ben Case studied Glen Strange with narrow curiosity. Glen could only shrug in reply.

The house had been cleaned up some since Glen had last entered it. Nora, taking the lead, led the party into what had apparently been J. Pierce Buchanan's office. There was a long walnut table surrounded by carved wooden chairs, a red brick fireplace and a portrait of a man with intense blue eyes and a full white beard gazing down on the assembled.

Craig Dumont made his way to the head of the table, adjusted his spectacles and opened the leather case he had been carrying. The three heirs gathered in the nearest chairs, Amanda on one side of the table, her brothers on the opposite. Nora and Ben Case, looking uneasy, sat a little farther away. Glen Strange, who found himself there only by whim, stood near the fireplace, arm on the mantle, watching.

He had not gotten a good look at the Buchanan brothers before, so now he measured them. The older, Earl was tall and narrow, with a lean tanned face. He had removed his planter's hat to show a shock of dark curly hair. Charles, his younger brother, wore a drab blue suit and a narrow tie. His eyes wandered from point to point as if he were uncomfortable here. Amanda, her bonnet removed, had not had the time to arrange her hair and blond tresses escaped their pins and ribbon and fell attractively across her shoulders.

'This is a somewhat complex will,'

Craig Dumont was saying, 'despite the simple bequests.' He took a deep breath and scratched idly at the spider-shaped scar on his cheek. He looked at those gathered around the table and then began to read from the paper before him.

'Insomuch — '

Earl Buchanan interrupted almost instantly. 'Look, here, Dumont,' he said in his lushly accented Mississippi drawl, 'none of us here is a lawyer. I would appreciate it, and I suspect everyone else would, if you'd skip all of that language you people use only to obfuscate or to edify your profession, and get to the nub of the matter. That is: what does it say absent the words that no one else on this planet but lawyers use?'

'You wish me to paraphrase?' Dumont asked, looking heated beneath his pallor. He glanced at the others, who nodded.

'Very well. There is a reason these documents are couched in such language, Mr Buchanan. In case of challenges to them — ' He abandoned

his lecture and said, 'Very well.' Unhappily, he scanned the last will and testament of J. Pierce Buchanan to re-familiarize himself with its terms. 'Here is what we have — according to the last wishes of the deceased. His property is to be divided thusly:

'The chief asset, of course, is the J-Bar Ranch the value of which cannot be accurately estimated at the present time.'

'Who gets it?' Charles asked. He was as impatient as his brother, it seemed, though he didn't have the same strength of personality.

'This is where the will becomes complicated,' Dumont said. 'If you had allowed me to read the specifics in the form with which they were recorded — '

'Who?' Earl Buchanan pressed, with more force. Craig Dumont sighed, touched his scar again and said directly:

'The J-Bar is to fall to whomsoever assumes residency. That is — '

'I know what that is!' Earl Buchanan said with frustration. 'You mean that

any of us willing to stay out West inherits the J-Bar?'

'Yes. Of course, if two of you — or all three of you — choose to remain on the ranch, the property will be so divided.'

'We have a plantation in Mississippi to run!' Earl said heatedly.

'Earl and I cannot possibly abandon our holdings there,' his brother agreed. The two let their eyes meet briefly.

'Well, then — ' Dumont hesitated.

'I'll stay,' Amanda said suddenly and the hostile eyes of the Buchanan brothers swept toward her.

'You can't!' Charles stuttered.

'Of course I can,' Amanda said. Her voice was cheerful, but there was spite in her eyes. 'Mother's dead. I have nothing in Ohio.'

'Then we get nothing! After the long trek out here?' Charles said dismally. He looked to his older brother for help.

'Wait,' Dumont said soothingly. 'That's not all there is to it. The J-Bar is, of course, the main bequeathed asset — '

He was rudely interrupted again.

'Why can't we sell it,' Charles interrupted, 'and split the money?'

'There's nothing to prevent that,' the lawyer answered, 'if all three of you were to reach an agreement. But — '

Ben Case spoke for the first time. 'You can't sell it,' the ranch foreman said. The Buchanan brothers turned angry eyes toward the uninvited speaker. Case lifted a hand and explained, 'That is, you could try. But a place of this size, there plain aren't many people who could afford it. Not men that know ranching.'

'First, of course, we would have to have the land and stock appraised,' Dumont advised the Buchanans. 'That would take some time. Then, as Case has pointed out, trying to find someone wanting a holding as vast as J-Bar, and having the money to purchase it, well, it would be a long while on the market, I'm afraid.'

'How long?' Earl Buchanan wanted to know.

'Months, a year — '

'More likely many years,' Ben Case said.

Scowling, Earl Buchanan snapped at Case, 'You don't want it sold because of your position here.'

Ben Case's dark face grew darker with displeasure. 'I got along before I rode onto J-Bar, I'll get along when it's gone,' he replied.

'We can't wait that long!' Charles wailed to his brother. 'If we don't return with cash money . . . it's the only reason we're here, of course. We've trouble with our holdings back home. The rice crop failed and now it looks if the indigo won't do as well as we'd hoped. If we could sell J-Bar quickly, even at a loss — '

'I don't want to sell the J-Bar,' Amanda put in, a little smugly, Glen Strange thought. 'I've considered it. I want to stay here. I am perfectly happy to accept the ranch as my inheritance.'

'Why you — ' Earl seemed ready to explode. He stiffened and half-rose from his chair. Craig Dumont calmed

him by lifting a hand.

'You never let me finish,' the lawyer said. He continued, 'In the event that the ranch proper falls to a single heir, the others are to share in the residual of J. Pierce's estate. 'All properties and monies not directly apportioned to the J-Bar Ranch'.'

'What the hell does that mean?' Earl asked, still angry. It was Nora who spoke now. She said:

'The fifty thousand in gold.'

'What fifty thousand?' Charles asked, his face hopeful and doubtful at once. 'Where is this money supposed to be?'

Glen Strange managed to speak up. '*That* is the question, isn't it?'

4

'So we're going to have a lady boss now?' Bobby Trapp asked in the morning as he and Glen Strange took their turn guarding Mae Buchanan's mausoleum. Another attempt to break into the tomb had occurred overnight. Two riders with axes and sledge hammers had to be driven off at gunpoint. Now the sun, risen but still screened by the oak grove, scattered red-gold across the face of the marble monument. Shadows were long; dew still sparkled on the grass. Doves had taken to wing, flying past toward their morning feeding sites.

'If she stays on,' Glen said. 'I had the idea that Amanda might have just been goading her brothers with that talk. She was still upset that they ran off and left her at the mercy of those highwaymen.'

'I don't blame her,' Bobby Trapp

said, lifting his eyes to watch a passing horseman. Neither of them recognized the rider. 'If she does stay, it might be interesting, though. Tell me, Glen did you ever work for a woman before?'

'Don't you remember the Pigeon-hole? Meg Bannister's place?'

Bobby frowned thoughtfully. 'Yes, I do, now that you mention it. We didn't last long there, did we? I'd forgotten that. I don't think I was even exactly sure that Meg was a female.'

One corner of Glen's mouth lifted in a smile. Bobby was right. With Amanda Buchanan no one would ever have to guess what sex she was. She was definitely a pretty girl, though she seemed temperamental and it was doubtful that she knew anything about cattle ranching. He supposed that didn't matter so long as Ben Case stayed on to manage the J-Bar. One of the stipulations in the will was that Ben Case was not to be dismissed for any reason so long as the J-Bar was not sold.

There was one other point that had caused Glen to wonder. *If* the ranch was sold, the house itself and a surrounding twenty acres were to fall to Nora. Each of the heirs had argued these and other points of the legacy for one reason or the other, but in the end Craig Dumont reminded them that those were the terms of the will and they had no grounds to dispute it.

'So now those two brothers are going to have to find their inheritance by poking around and digging holes like the rest of the vultures?' Bobby Trapp asked.

'So it seems,' Glen Strange answered. He was back to wondering if someone — Nora, perhaps — hadn't already found the hidden gold and re-hidden it in a private place where no one could ever discover it. Or simply ridden into the town of Big Springs and deposited it until all of the fuss had died down. He also wondered again about the relationship between Nora and Ben Case, although it was none of his

business. Maybe the two had worked out the plan in the days following J. Pierce's murder. Which brought Glen's circular thoughts back to their starting point.

'It still seems that there's no one even trying to find out who murdered the old man, Bobby.'

'Not so's you could notice it.'

'He's murdered and their first and only thought is on how much it profits them.'

Bobby nodded, 'Doesn't say much for us as a race, does it?'

'If someone shot down your grandfather — ' Glen began and then he remembered that someone had shot down Bobby's father on the streets of Billings, Montana, and Bobby had ridden the man down after a three-month hunt.

'I wonder,' Bobby Trapp said, nodding toward the tomb they were now guarding, 'if the old man didn't put the gold in here after all.'

'No, I don't think he did,' Glen

Strange said. 'Look at what's happened since he died. Must be two dozen men who've tried to break into it. J. Pierce was a smart man; he would have seen that coming. He hid it well, but he hid it where his children can find it but no one else can.'

'And where, Glen, might that be?'

Glen half-smiled again. He had no idea.

Nor did anyone else, but it didn't stop them from coming. By noon he and Bobby had counted another ten men lurking near the tomb or slipping through the oaks trees, none of them having a better idea than Glen Strange did about where the gold might be hidden. Glen supposed that the simple fact that they were now guarding the mausoleum might have re-enforced the notion that that was where the gold had been hidden.

By noon, both Bobby and Glen were tired of sentry duty. They were not soldiers used to standing watch, but cowboys, and a day out of the saddle

was like a day lost. For Glen at least, the monotony was to end soon.

'Here comes Tiny,' Bobby Trapp said early in the afternoon. He was standing so that the shadow of one of the cherubs fell across his face. 'Hope he's got our dinner with him.'

Glen, glancing that way, saw the white-haired man walking toward them with a parcel wrapped in brown paper in his hands. It was about the size two meals would require. Arriving, Tiny handed the package to Bobby.

'Only ham and bread again, Bobby, but I brought you plenty.'

'Suits me,' Bobby Trapp said, looking around for a place to sit down.

'You, Glen, they want over at the big house.'

'What for?'

'I wouldn't know. Ask them. You're supposed to report to the new boss lady,' Tiny said with a sly smile he could not hide.

Amanda herself greeted Glen at the door to the big house. She was wearing

a yellow dress this afternoon and a white bonnet with a yellow ribbon around it.

'Oh, good, you're here,' Amanda said, not stepping aside to allow him to enter, but walking out onto the porch, closing the heavy door behind her.

'What is it you needed?' Glen asked uncertainly. He tipped back his hat and let his gray eyes carefully, but he hoped not intrusively, study the little blond woman. Her eyes were eager, her lips pursed, her cheeks flushed with subdued excitement.

'You're going to take me into town. Big Springs. Ben Case already has the buckboard hitched.'

'Mind if I ask why we're going? And why me?' he asked. She was already on her way, stepping down the three steps to the yard, heading toward the red barn, her chin uplifted.

'I have to collect the rest of my belongings at the freight office, now that I know I'll be staying on here. As for asking you to drive, well, who else is

there? Craig Dumont left at first light and my brothers, even if I wanted to ask one of them to take me, are busy going through grandfather's desk and papers, looking for clues to the missing gold.

'You showed yourself to be a man yesterday. If those bandits . . . And there might very well be more of them prowling around from what you say. I have little enough, but nothing I can afford to lose.' Glen only nodded.

Beside the barn, a dour-faced Ben Case crouched in the shade, holding the reins to the two-horse team. He rose at their approach, touched his hat brim to Amanda Buchanan and handed the reins to Glen with a gloved hand. Glen briefly double-checked the harnesses, which caused Ben's frown to deepen. Amanda was handed aboard the wagon and they started on their way.

Clearing the ranch yard, Glen felt a sense of relief he could not define. The J-Bar seemed an unhealthy place to be.

Maybe it was that, maybe it was the clean fresh air flowing past them as they drove that invigorated him. Or simply the presence of the pretty little blonde at his side. The willows along the creek were silver-green in the afternoon light, the creek deep blue. Higher along the mountain slopes was a golden flourish of aspen and deep blue-green Douglas fir trees.

'You shouldn't hold yesterday against your brothers,' Glen said as he slowed the team at a creek crossing. 'They were unarmed and taken by surprise.'

'They weren't unarmed,' Amanda said. 'I saw a pistol under Earl's coat. They were just cowardly. Look at you and your friend. Pursuing the outlaws. I'll never forget it,' It seemed, however, that she already had.

'That was just Bobby doing the pursuing, Miss Buchanan. If you'll remember. That's his way. He's got a streak of hot blood in him. Me, I'm just sort of plagued with ... cool disregard.'

Amanda glanced at him with amusement. 'That's a funny way to put it,' she said.

'I thought so myself,' Glen admitted. 'Bobby said something like that to me the other day. I've been trying since to figure out exactly what he meant by it.'

The buckboard achieved the flats again and rumbled on toward Big Springs, the horses moving easily. 'You and Bobby have been friends for a long time?' Amanda asked.

'Yes, Miss, for some time now. We've bounced around from job to job. There's a lot of ranches scattered around Colorado now, but only a few of them are flourishing. Mostly we find work at roundup time and spend the rest of the year just dragging the line.'

'What does that mean? 'Dragging the line'?'

Glen told her, 'Just wandering from ranch to ranch, looking for whatever work might need done. Chopping wood, pitching hay, busting broncs — whatever we can find.'

73

'Well, you won't have to worry about that anymore, will you?' Amanda said brightly. 'I mean, J-Bar needs steady, reliable hands. You've got a job as long as you want one. You and Bobby both.'

'Well thank you, Miss, but — '

'But a part of the bargain is that you have to quit calling me 'miss',' she laughed. 'I might be your boss-lady, but we can still be friends. Call me Amanda, please.'

'All right. Speaking of reliable men, you're still short on trustworthy hands . . . Amanda. Outside of me, Bobby and the Fain brothers, Tiny says there's no one left around that you can count on.'

'Not at present, from what they tell me,' she agreed. She frowned slightly, her eyes fixed on him. 'Why do you bring that up now?'

'Just this — we've got a swarm of fortune hunters on the property now. Broke and frustrated. Sooner or later they're going to give up on this search for hidden gold, but they'll still be broke, frustrated and troublesome.'

'So you think — '

'I think at that point they're going to start looking around for the next source of easy cash, and with a lot of your former cowhands among them, they're naturally going to turn their thoughts to your cattle herds.'

'You think they'll turn to rustling?' Amanda replied.

'I think they'll have to. Those runaway soldiers can't just ride back to their post and turn themselves in. Your cowboys already know they won't be rehired. Tiny made that clear to me. A man hates to be frustrated in his quest, Amanda. They'll want something to show for their efforts. If not gold, why then something just as good — money on the hoof.'

'Maybe Ben Case knows where we can hire some other responsible men,' Amanda said. 'I'll talk to him about it.'

'I would,' Glen Strange agreed. Ahead now the indistinct shapes of the buildings forming the town of Big Springs were visible. Their way now led

across open grassland without any concealing timber stands. Inwardly Glen breathed a sigh of relief. There were still robbers lurking and he had ridden the last few miles with his eyes alert, his pistol at the ready.

The town rested lazily under cool skies and bright sunlight. There was little industry and more idlers than Glen would have expected to see. Amanda directed him to the freight office which sat next to the train depot. A locomotive puffing smoke sat straddling the silver rails in front of the white-painted buildings. Glen guided the team behind the freight office and looped the reins around the brake handle. He waited, arms folded, leaning against the buckboard while Amanda went in to find out about her shipped baggage.

Returning she told him, 'It's only just come in on that train out in front. It'll be an hour or two before they've unloaded the train and sorted my trunks out.'

'All right. I'll take care of the horses in the meantime.'

'Do that,' she said, 'and then why don't you take care of yourself. I know you missed your lunch. Maybe you should at least get a sandwich and a beer somewhere.'

The suggestion was a welcome one and after handing the horses over to a short-term stable to be cooled, fed and watered, Glen started up a dusty street, looking for a restaurant or saloon. A saloon, he decided would be easier and quicker than a sit-down café, so long as they had a counter lunch.

He didn't have to search long. The saloon had no name attached to it that Glen could see, but it was filled with the buzz of men drinking, talking, playing cards, idling away the day. There was a lunch of roast beef and cheese along with some yeasty bread that was going dry around the edges, all free for the price of a mug of beer, and after ordering one Glen helped himself to lunch. As full as the saloon was, the

only place to eat was standing at the bar, jostled by elbows and hips as men squeezed past. To his left a sloppy-looking fat man was served and given his change by the harried bartender.

Glen could hear snatches of conversation along the bar. One man was saying loudly, 'Look at what's happening around here! All these drifters with nothing to do. They'll stoop to robbery next, you can count on it. I tell you a change is going to be made when the election for sheriff comes up next year. Can you beat old Fowler leaving for Arizona just when we needed him most.'

'Ed!' the big man beside Glen Strange yelled out sharply. 'What the hell's this supposed to be?'

The bartender glanced back, wiping his hands on his apron. Squinting at the coin the angry fat man was holding up, he shrugged an apology.

'Sorry, Nate,' the bartender apologized. Interested, Glen glanced at the change the big man held in his palm.

'What is that, anyway?' he asked.

'It's a French coin,' the bartender said, exchanging it. Nate muttered, 'I ain't a Frenchman. I'd like my change in American money.'

Glen halted the bartender. 'What did you say that was?'

'A florin, took it by mistake. We get them sometimes from men traveling out of the Deep South. They still use them in some parts of Louisiana, though the French sold that land to us a long time ago. I sometimes get stuck with pesos, too. Just the other night . . . '

Glen paid no attention to the rest of the bartender's lament. A *florin*? Probably from down Louisiana way.

Traveling through Louisiana was the only way to get west from the state of Mississippi. The Buchanan brothers would have come that way. Interrupting the bartender, Glen asked: 'Any idea who might have slipped that French coin to you?'

'Mister, look around this place. On Saturday nights we've twice this many

customers jammed in here. Half the people in town are strangers. I have no idea.' He was summoned by a pair of cowboys drinking farther along the bar. Glen finished sipping his beer, pondering matters.

He wondered just how long the Buchanans had really been in town. Were they newly arrived or only pretending that they were? Had they been here, for example, long enough to have been in the area when J. Pierce Buchanan was murdered? Their baggage did not necessarily have to have just arrived on yesterday's train. Baggage can be stored.

For that matter, he realized, Amanda Buchanan's luggage could have been stored for days, weeks at the freight office. She told him that it had just arrived on today's train, but he had not gone inside with her when she was told that, and she had been quick to shoo him away from the place. He didn't like that idea, but a man had to wonder.

If he had the time he could ask

around at the hotels and find out if Earl and Charles Buchanan — or Amanda — had been staying in town. It seemed that the lawyer would have known, but maybe not. Perhaps they were all playing a part in some bloody charade.

Glen placed his empty mug down on the polished counter of the bar and went out of the saloon, his spirits much lower than when he had entered.

Feeling vaguely disloyal, Glen returned to the stable and reclaimed the team and buckboard. Amanda was waiting for him when he reached the freight office, a neat stack of luggage beside her. He placed her trunks in the back of the wagon and helped her up onto the bench seat of the buckboard. She was smiling prettily when Glen took his own place beside her, but his mood was dour. His thinking had led him down paths of uncertainty.

'What happened to you?' Amanda asked after they had passed the outskirts of Big Springs and began following the long trail home. 'Is

something troubling you, Glen?'

'I'm just thinking,' he said without looking at her. The horses carried them on at an even pace, their tails lifted, ears pricked with energetic alertness. The creek flowed silver-blue, winding its way through the willows.

'What's bothering you, really?' she persisted.

Raising his expressionless gray eyes, he told her. 'I'm still thinking about something that doesn't seem to be troubling anyone else around here. I mean to solve it, Amanda.' His voice carried a shadow of dark intent. 'I intend to find out who murdered J. Pierce Buchanan.'

Amanda's lips parted, her eyes filled with surprise. She would have spoken, but at that moment the guns opened up from the willow trees.

5

The first rifle bullet whined off the buckboard's metalwork not two feet from where Glen sat. Singing off the iron strap, the slug ricocheted madly away. Before they could turn their heads to glance at the pursuing riders, three more shots were fired, none of them striking flesh, none missing by much. The two bandits must have been hiding in the willow brush planning their ambush. Glen cursed himself for not being alert enough to notice them, but really the brush was so thick that an army could have been hidden there unseen.

Glenn's inattentiveness caused one of the wagon wheels to hit a large rock and the buckboard jolted high in the air, unseating both of them. Glen cursed and settled the horses into a run. Their strides were long and

unlabored, but the saddle ponies would catch up quick enough. Amanda's bonnet had been dislodged and it now hung on its tie ribbon down her back. She gripped the wagon seat with both hands, her eyes wide.

Ahead the road looped back on itself, following the meandering creek's course. Glen made a hasty decision.

'Can you handle the team?' he shouted at the panicked Amanda Buchanan.

'I can drive, but — '

'Good.' Glen thrust the reins in her direction and told her. 'As soon as we're around the bend, run the team another hundred yards, then pull up. Tell them that one of their shots got me.'

'Let them catch me!' Amanda shouted in protest. She was fitting the ribbons of leather around her fingers. 'What will they do? Glen, where are you going!'

There was no time to explain further. As the wagon swept around the bend

they were briefly concealed by the creek-side brush and Glen rose, crouched and leaped from the buckboard, rolling into the screen the willows formed. Seconds later the two pursuing men pounded past on their horses, but they did not glance his way.

Glen was to his feet, fighting his way through the underbrush. Reaching the creek bed he sprinted toward the point ahead where the road completed its loop and straightened out again, heading toward the J-Bar. The sun flickered through the trees, the river stones underfoot were round and slick. Glen ran on, his pistol in hand, his heart thumping heavily, his lungs heated.

Splashing across the shallow creek he again entered the willows and emerged onto the trail not thirty feet from where the bandits had halted Amanda and the buckboard. One of the men sat his horse beside the woman, holding the reins to the team while the other, who had clambered up into the bed of the wagon, unloaded Amanda's trunks.

He could hear her complaining. 'There's nothing in there but a woman's clothes!'

They paid no attention. They were probably hoping to find the missing gold, but they would be satisfied with anything valuable they could find. One of the leather trunks was broken open and the bandit was crouched over them, pawing through Amanda's clothing.

'There's nothing worth the having here, Hilgers,' Glen Strange heard the man say. 'This was a bad idea.'

'A very bad idea,' Glen Strange said behind him. The ear of his Colt .44 was drawn back, his finger curled around the cool steel of the trigger. The mounted outlaw had his second bad idea of the day.

And his last.

The horseman still held his Winchester in his free hand. Now he dropped the reins to the team that he had been holding and lifted his long gun to his shoulder. It was an easy shot for Glen

Strange. His revolver bucked in his hand as he put two bullets into the bandit. The dead man was still tumbling from his horse when the second man made his move.

The robber, who had been searching through Amanda's goods, had placed his rifle on the tailgate of the buckboard. He glanced toward it once and then went for his belt gun instead. He was slow and very awkward. Glen Strange was braced and ready. Before the ambusher's gun could come up to waist level, Strange pulled his trigger again and the man took lead, staggering back against the buckboard. He struck the tailgate and fell to the dark earth, his pistol held uselessly in his limp fingers.

'Is he . . . are they?' Amanda asked excitedly. She was standing in the buckboard's box, staring back toward Glen Strange.

'Let's hope so,' Glen said, kicking the pistol out of the dead man's hand. Slowly he circled toward the rifleman

whose faithful pony stood over him, head hanging. Crouching, Glen quickly felt for a pulse, fanned the man's pockets and rose to show Amanda what he had found. The brass deputy sheriff's star shone dully in the sunlight, completing Po Hilgers' posthumous introduction.

'He was one of the deputy sheriffs,' Glen told Amanda. He motioned for her to collect the reins and get the excited buckboard team under control.

'You killed a lawman?' she asked a little hysterically.

'He wasn't even lawman enough to wear his badge,' Glen said. Curling his finger around the edge of the badge, he sent it sailing toward the creek. He returned to the back of the wagon, roughly repacked Amanda's dresses and assorted frillery and heaved the trunks back onto the wagon bed.

Clambering back up into the wagon box he accepted the reins from Amanda's trembling hands and asked, 'Are you ready to return home?'

'I'm ready to never leave J-Bar again,' she said and her voice squeaked a little. She readjusted her bonnet, folded her hands in her lap and sat silently as Glen Strange started the team, guiding it once more toward the home ranch.

'You did what?' Bobby Trapp asked with surprise as the two stood just inside the barn. Glen had finished unharnessing the buckboard team, rubbing the horses down and putting them away in their stalls.

'I shot a deputy sheriff. The one we hadn't met. Po Hilgers, if you remember the name.'

'That might mean trouble for you, Glen,' Bobby said in a low voice.

'It might. I'm telling you so that you'll know,' Glenn answered, 'but it's best if no one else hears about it.'

'You know me, Glen. I won't say a word, but what about the girl?'

'I think I impressed upon Amanda how inconvenient it would be for me if anyone found out about it.'

'You *think*?' Bobby Trapp said worriedly.

'If — ' Glen's words broke off as the shadow of a man standing in the doorway fell across the straw-littered floor. Both glanced that way to see Ben Case standing there, hands on his hips, studying them. His badly pocked face was set in its habitual scowl.

'What is it, Case?' Glen Strange asked.

'You boys saddle your horses and pick up some supplies from Tiny. The Fain boys have been down on the south range for three nights running. They could use a night sleeping off the ground.'

'All right,' Glen said amiably. After all, there was no one else around to relieve the Fains.

'Strange,' Ben Case said in a cool voice. 'J-Bar might have a new owner, but I'm still the one who gives the orders around here. Do you understand me?'

Glen only nodded his answer. After

the foreman had gone, Bobby Trapp asked, 'What do you think that was about?'

'The man was just asserting his authority,' Glen answered as he tightened the cinch on his saddle.

'I suppose so,' Bobby said. 'But it seemed kind of unnecessary.'

Glen led his gray horse across the yard toward the bunkhouse. Bobby Trapp walked his sleek roan beside him. Tiny was in the doorway of the building, a canvas sack of provisions at his feet.

'Someone's watching,' Bobby commented, and Glen Strange looked across his shoulder to see Amanda Buchanan, arms folded, watching them as they walked their horses through the oak trees. He did not wave; neither did she. 'The J-Bar still isn't your normal ranch,' Bobby Trapp said. 'I get edgy around here. I wonder if those two brothers of hers have gone yet.'

They asked Tiny that question, and the white-haired man told them, 'No. I

seen them pacing around the outside of the house. I couldn't tell if they were looking for something or just talking away from the others.'

Bobby lost the coin flip and so they tied the awkward provision sack onto his saddle. The horses, well-rested now, moved out eagerly past the oaks and onto the long-grass meadows beyond. Glen was starting to envy the Fain Brothers. Two nights in a cot with a roof above him had already spoiled him. Tonight would find them back where they had spent almost every night of the last few years — beneath the sky, hoping that it did not rain, hoping that the cattle were in a placid mood, that there were no coyotes, wolves or pumas prowling.

And no other predators. There was an abundance of the human kind still in evidence on the J-Bar land. They happened to pass three other unknown men who were standing in the shade of a sycamore tree, doing nothing what-ever that Glen and Bobby Trapp could

tell except watching back.

'Sooner or later someone's going to come up with the idea of cutting out a few beeves,' Bobby said, and Glen agreed.

'Sooner or later.' He hoped that J-Bar would come by a few more trustworthy men before that happened. It was something he had wanted to discuss with Ben Case, but the foreman had seemed in no mood for conversation.

An hour on, the sun was already lowering toward the far, snow-capped mountains and dusk was settling in velvet pools. Riding through the scattered cedars and young blue spruce trees, they came upon Austin and Rod Fain sitting their horses side by side in a small hollow overlooking the cattle and a meandering rill.

'You boys are relieved,' Bobby Trapp said cheerfully.

Ron Fain answered, 'And only two days late.'

'There wasn't nobody around,' his brother, Austin, reminded him. 'Glad to

see you boys,' he told Bobby and Glen. 'We've got us a problem. Our youngest brother, Will, is missing. We haven't seen him since we got back from helping you push that last bunch of cattle.'

'Where do you think he could be?' Bobby asked.

'There's no telling. We looked down as far as the Honey Bear and over to Slate Ridge. No sign of him. Even if his horse went down and pinned him, Will would have fired distress shots to summon us. He's young, but he's been working the range for a long while. He would know we'd come running at that signal.'

'How can we help?' Glen asked.

'Well, I don't see how you can at all,' Austin had to tell them. 'You don't know the area and before long darkness is going to settle. All you can do is hope he walks in or fires signal shots.'

'We'll keep an eye out for him,' Bobby promised. 'And if we hear anything that sounds like distress shots,

we'll go looking.'

It was obvious that Austin and Rod were reluctant to leave, equally obvious that they could achieve nothing by remaining. As Austin had pointed out, darkness was descending rapidly over them. Eventually the worried pair started their ponies homeward as sunset stained the western sky with a flourish of bright color.

'What do you say, Glen? We ride once around the herd then come back to make a night camp?'

'I suppose so,' Glen answered heavily. 'Later, do you want first shift or should I take it?'

'I'll take first watch,' Bobby volunteered. 'You've had a rougher day than I had. All I did was march back and forth in front of that mausoleum.'

The night grew cool but not intolerably so. Glen smoothed out a patch of ground beneath twin blue spruce trees and rolled up into his blankets. Meanwhile, Bobby Trapp had ridden out to ride night herd, circling

the animals slowly as he rode, humming and sometimes singing softly to let the cows know that it was a man coming and not something to get spooked about. Riding herd on this many cattle was nearly pointless for two men. If the cattle ran there was no way they could hope to halt a stampede. But mainly they were keeping an eye out for would-be rustlers. These would be only a few disorganized men, Glen thought, but possibly desperate enough to shoot it out.

The bands of roving trespassers had no leaders, no need or desire for any, but as time went by with the chances of finding Buchanan's gold growing faint, they would turn to other pursuits and once organized and given direction, there seemed no way the J-Bar at its present strength could do anything to thwart the rustlers.

For the time being Glen let all of these thoughts dissipate. With a vast yawn he drew his body more tightly together for warmth against the night

chill and fell off to sleep, after a few wasted minutes in which he thought of the silken hair and merry blue eyes of Amanda Buchanan.

'How about it,' the man crouched beside Glen Strange muttered. It seemed from the impatience in his voice that it was not the first words he had spoken to Glen. 'Going to roll out so I can get some sleep too?' Bobby Trapp asked.

Glen sat up, rubbing an eye with his knuckle. 'Sorry, Bobby. I didn't know I was that tired.'

Bobby Trapp grinned, sat down and began prying his boots off. 'That's all right. It didn't take me more than twenty minutes to wake you up.'

'What time is it?'

'I read four o'clock by the stars.'

'Already! You should have wakened me earlier,' Glen said, getting to his feet, rolling his blanket up.

'I had mercy on you,' Bobby said with another smile as he tugged his Indian blanket up under his chin. 'You

owe me a small favor.'

Glen nodded his thanks again and walked to where his gray horse had been picketed. By the time he was saddled and aboard, Bobby Trapp was lost in deep sleep himself.

Glen Strange started his horse circling the herd, singing softly as he went. Starlight gleamed on the horns of the cattle. His gray pony left hoofprints in the thin veil of frost covering the grassy ground. The moon had faded early and was now only a faintly glowing memory behind the saw-toothed mountains to the far west. Glen dipped into the narrow valley which formed the southern extent of the J-Bar range to assure himself that none of the cattle had crossed the bordering creek. There were a few large sycamore trees growing there and scattered pine trees. The shadows were deep, cobalt blue and cold. The stars were reflected hazily in the ripples of the creek.

The man with the Winchester stepped into Glen's path and said softly, 'Hold

up a minute, will you?' Glen reined in his gray in deference to the rifle which was held in a manner that indicated a readiness to use it. One of the wandering treasure-hunters, Glen guessed.

He was wrong.

From the opposite side of the trail a second man, shorter, darker, emerged, also holding a rifle. This one took up a position slightly behind Glen. The man who had spoken came nearer, took the gray by its bridle and looked up at Glen Strange.

'You're not him.'

'No,' Glen replied, having no idea who the man with the rifle meant, but certain that he did not wish to be whoever it was that he was looking for. The night shadows concealed the stranger's face, but Glen had an impression of hawkish features and glittering, narrow eyes.

'What are you doing out here?' he asked Glen.

'I work here. I'm a J-Bar hand.'

'Oh?' the man peered even more

intently at Glen. 'Then you know Ben Case.'

'I know him, yes.'

'Tell him I want to see him. Tell him Wichita wants his cut.'

'Your cut?' Glen said to the man who was apparently this Wichita.

'That's right. Word got to me that Case has cut himself into an inheritance. Some old man died, isn't that right?' Glen nodded. 'They say Ben got something out of it. I want my share — he owes me.'

'I'll tell him,' Glen agreed, lifting one shoulder in a shrug. 'Is that all? Just 'Wichita wants his cut'?'

'Tell him where I am. Tell him that I'm waiting to see him.'

'All right,' Glen said. He wasn't about to question the gunman further. He would agree to whatever he said. The man with the rifle stepped back and Glen assumed that the conversation was over, but Wichita spoke again.

'You know who Ben Case really is?' he asked. Before Glen could speak,

Wichita answered his own question. 'He's a wanted man still. He's done his share of killing. No matter that he's ridden this far and hidden this long. They still want him for a hanging offense. I can give the law all they need to know to make sure that they finally catch up with Ben Case.'

This was said not with anger, but with bitter certainty. 'You used to ride with Case, then?'

For a moment Glen thought Wichita would not answer, but he did. 'I rode with him, sided with him in more than one fight. What thanks did I get for it? When the chips were down Ben rode off and left me. I was doing time in prison while he was out here a free man.'

Glen didn't say anything. He didn't know Ben Case well. Neither did he think it was a good idea to tell Wichita that so far as he knew Case had gotten nothing but a promise of lifelong employment from J. Pierce Buchanan's bequest. Wichita was not shouting,

threatening, or cursing, but there was a sort of implacable menace about him. Glen had no wish to stir things up.

'I won't see Case for at least another day,' he told Wichita. 'But when I do, I'll be sure to give him your message.'

'You do that,' Wichita said coldly. 'Another day doesn't matter after the years I've already waited. You just make sure you tell him that I'm waiting.'

Then he slowly backed away, turned his back to Glen and walked into the shadows of the trees. Glancing behind him, Glen saw that the other man had already vanished. Glen heeled his gray and turned its head up out of the gully. He wanted to get as far away from Wichita and his friend as possible, and quickly.

The rest of the night he rode speculating on Wichita and Ben Case, on Nora and on Earl and Charles Buchanan, on Amanda and the lawyer, Craig Dumont. Each of them had an individual program in place but Glen didn't know enough to figure out what

they all were, and he was not so certain that it would be healthy to know.

He was hungry and saddle-weary by the time the sun lazily lifted its head from the dark line of the eastern horizon, and he turned the gray horse back toward the camp. Bobby was already up, crouched over a low fire he was building to boil coffee.

'You didn't sleep much,' Glen commented as he swung down from his horse.

'I don't need much, Glen.' Bobby's eyes wore an unhappy expression and his mouth was turned down just a little. 'I ran across something while I was gathering dry wood for the fire.'

'Oh?' Glen frowned. If Bobby Trapp was this upset, it was truly bad news. Bobby rose, dusted his hands on his jeans and inclined his head toward the heavier forest beyond the camp.

'This way,' Bobby said, starting toward the scattered pines.

The shallow grave had been disturbed by wild things. The young man

with the flaxen hair lay crumpled there, one leg and one arm unearthed. It was — had to be — Will Fain. Glen breathed a curse, going nearer the dead man.

'There's a bullet hole behind his ear,' Bobby Trapp said quietly. 'Whoever did it intended to make sure he was dead.'

'Did you find his horse?' Glen asked. Men had been killed for less.

'No,' Bobby answered. 'But you don't think — '

'Not really,' Glen said. He did not really believe that a roving man afoot had killed Will Fain just for his horse. Not the way it had been done.

'Damn this ranch!' Bobby said bitterly. 'Glen, we came here to try to find some work, to rest ourselves and our ponies. The J-Bar is an unholy tangle. If we had any sense we'd just ride out of here before one or the other of us gets shot as well.'

'It's a mess, all right,' Glen said with one last glance at the body of Will Fain. 'And I agree, there's more trouble to

come. Let's sit down and discuss it, Bobby. I need to tell you what happened to me last night.'

'Something else?' Bobby shook his head heavily. 'All right, Glen. Let's talk. Mind if we have us a cup of coffee while we do that?' They started slowly back through the pines, the new sun brilliant in their eyes, the scent of the pines lush and fragrant. Out on the long grass the cattle were stirring sleepily.

Around the scarcely burning campfire they stood away from the smoke and sipped at the strong black coffee while Glen told him about the encounter with the man named Wichita. Bobby stood looking toward the stirring herd, coffee cup in hand, his hat tipped back.

'We've got to figure something out, Glen,' he was saying. 'I don't like all this wandering around in the dark. The thing is too complicated for a simple man like me. We've at least got this morning to figure out what we want to

do. Nothing else can happen to us for a while.'

Even as he spoke, the sound of arriving hoof beats scattered that confidence. A rider on a pale horse was making his way toward their camp.

6

The rider was a dark silhouette approaching the camp from out of the yellow-orange globe of the rising sun. Bobby Trapp switched his coffee cup to his left hand and placed his right on the handle of his holstered Colt .44 revolver.

'Easy, Bobby,' Glen cautioned, for he had identified the rider. As she passed from the deep shadows of the pines into the sunlight so did Bobby Trapp. It was hard to mistake the shining golden hair of Amanda Buchanan. She slowed her horse and walked the high-stepping blue roan toward them. There was no smile on her face.

'I need you, Glen,' she blurted out as the impatient horse tossed its head and stamped. Glen stepped forward, taking the horse's bridle to calm it.

'What's the matter?' he asked her.

The excitement in Amanda's blue eyes matched that of the spirited roan.

'I want you back at the house. There's something going on that I don't understand and it's frightening me. There's no one to watch out for me there.'

'There's Ben Case,' Glen Strange said.

'I think he's part of it,' she said nervously.

'Part of what?' he asked the half-hysterical woman.

'That's just it, Glen, I'm not sure. It has something to do with the codicil to the will — that's what they call it, isn't it? The added conditions.'

'I think so,' Glen answered. 'But I don't understand. What codicil?'

'Dumont waited until you had gone. You, Nora and Ben Case. It was only for the family's ears,' he told us.

'And it stipulated?' Glen inquired. What could have made the woman so excited, so fearful?

'Earl and Charles were angry. Very angry — '

He had to interrupt her. 'What did the lawyer tell them, Amanda?'

'They have to remain on the J-Bar for another three weeks or they inherit nothing.'

'Why, I wonder,' Glen said. He had no way of knowing. He didn't know how J. Pierce's mind had worked. The old man must have had his reasons, but what they were was a mystery.

'I don't know,' Amanda said in confusion. More calmly, she added, 'I would guess that after three weeks Dumont is going to tell them where the fifty thousand is hidden, wouldn't you?'

'It's a good guess,' Glen agreed, 'as far as it goes. But I still don't see why are you so excited, Amanda.'

'Excited! You'd be too. There are people prowling around the house in the dead of night. I hear their footsteps outside my room. I keep my door bolted now. Last night I heard someone trying the doorknob.'

'Are you sure?' Glen asked the

overexcited woman.

'Yes, I am sure,' she said as if speaking to a child. 'When I went out into the hallway to check there was no one there but Nora clutching her robe. She said she thought she had heard someone too, but I'm pretty sure it was her who tried my door.'

'You could have too much imagination,' Glen said and Amanda's expression darkened petulantly. Then he asked, 'Why do you say you suspect Ben Case is involved?'

'After Nora went back into her room, I returned to mine. But I waited there awhile with the door open a crack. I heard a man's voice in Nora's room, Glen. I'm sure of it. And it had to be Ben Case's.'

'I can see that this is frightening, confusing,' Glen said, 'but I can't ride back with you just now. Bobby and I have work to do out here.'

'Yes, and Ben Case is the one who sent you out here,' Amanda said pointedly.

'Yes, and — '

'Yes, and this ranch is mine, not his, Glen Strange. *I* am the one who gives the orders here. If I have to order you to return to the ranch with me, then that's what I'm doing.'

'Then there's no choice, is there?' Glen said. The woman had starch, it seemed. 'That means the Fain brothers will have to come back out here to ride herd.'

Bobby Trapp spoke up for the first time, 'Better have 'em bring an extra horse.' Amanda's eyes flickered questioningly toward the cowboy.

'What for? What do you mean?'

Glen told her, 'We found Will Fain. Someone's murdered him.'

'Will Fain?' Amanda looked blank.

He had forgotten that she hadn't had the time to even meet the Fain brothers. He told her, 'Their youngest brother. He was killed up here yesterday.'

'Was it an accident?' Amanda asked, trembling slightly. She knew what the

answer would be even before Glen gently took her hand and shook his head. Amanda said, 'Will you tell them, Glen? I don't even know the men.'

'I hardly know them myself, but yes I'll tell them. We're still going to be short of men out here unless Ben Case has figured out where we can hire some new hands.'

Amanda's temper flared again. 'He won't have! And even if he did, I don't want anyone he would hire working on the J-Bar.'

'I've a suggestion,' Bobby Trapp put in. 'You know that before, when some of your hands have come back tired and disgusted from the pointless search for your grandfather's gold, they've found their bunks cleared and their mats rolled up. Tiny said that Case told him just to fire every single one of them. It seems to me that some of those men must have been good hands who just got caught up in things, and might now feel properly ashamed of the way they behaved. Maybe it wouldn't be such a

bad idea to take some of them back on. A kind of amnesty.'

'You may be right,' Amanda considered. 'They didn't really do anything that terrible. I'll talk to Tiny about it. If he gives a man his thumbs-up, I'll let him re-hire him.' Glen nodded his agreement. It wasn't a bad idea, though he noticed that she was giving the decision-making to Tiny and not to Ben Case. That was sure to rankle the J-Bar foreman.

Amanda told Bobby, 'When the Fain brothers ride out here, they are to stay. Bobby can bring the . . . Will back to the ranch.'

'All right,' Bobby agreed. 'Unless the Fains have some objection to doing things that way.'

Amanda turned her eyes to Glen. 'You had better saddle up. We're going to ride back to town.'

Surprised, Glen asked her, 'What for?'

'I am going to talk to Craig Dumont again. He read the entire will, but he's

not telling all he knows. I want to find out if that fifly thousand does exist, and if it does, discover why it can't be given to my brothers immediately. They are a nuisance around the ranch, poking around here and there. Going through my grandfather's papers — again! I even saw them looking at Mae Buchanan's grave themselves as if they, like everyone else, thought it might hold the treasure. I want them off the place, gone back to Mississippi. Earl is in a rage. He says that this year's crops will be ruined if he doesn't get back to Mississippi immediately and see to the harvesting. He only came out here to get the money to save his plantation, now he's in more danger of losing it to his creditors.'

With seeming irrelevance Glen asked as he shouldered his saddle, 'Where did you and your brothers join up, Amanda?'

'You mean on the trip west?' she asked with surprise. 'Not until we reached Big Springs. They were on the

train that arrived the day before mine. Why do you ask?'

'No reason,' Glen shrugged. He was still thinking about that French coin, the florin that someone had passed in the Big Springs saloon before any of them were supposed to have arrived in town. He had not told Bobby about that either, and so he also got a curious look from him. Glen saddled his gray horse, tugging the double cinches of his Texas-rigged saddle tight. It would be quicker to ride from where they were and pick up the trail to town, but they needed to advise the Fain brothers, and Glen Strange wanted to tell Case about this man, Wichita.

It would be interesting to see the look on the J-Bar foreman's face when he heard about him. Starting back through the scattered pines toward the ranch, Glen fell into silent thought. He did not necessarily share Amanda's conviction that there was a conspiracy against her, but too many unanswered — and unasked — questions remained.

One thing that puzzled him was why no one had heard the shots that killed J. Pierce Buchanan. Tiny had said that a pillow was used to muffle the sounds, and it was true that the bunkhouses were some distance from the main house, but surely anyone inside the house itself would have heard the disturbance. Where had Nora been all the time J. Pierce was being tortured and killed? What motive would she have had for being involved in any plot? Well, money obviously. Although she had a place to live and lifetime employment, that might not be enough for her if she had expected more.

And as far as Amanda's situation went, well, if she did not continue to live on the J-Bar, the house itself and twenty surrounding acres were to fall to Nora as her inheritance. Was that enough to provoke murder? People had been murdered for less, Glen reminded himself glumly.

He glanced at Amanda, whose smile

had returned, not so bright as previously, but it was there as she rode beside Glen Strange, her horse high-stepping energetically, the light breeze drifting her blonde hair.

'Did you ever wonder who left Nora on Grandfather's doorstep?' Amanda asked.

'It's crossed my mind.'

'I mean, way out here! It had to be someone who knew J-Bar and its owner, didn't it?'

'I would think so,' Glen answered, but he had no guess to offer. Between the two of them, they knew little, it seemed. *One thing at a time*, Glen told himself. That was the only way to go about handling the situation.

Reaching the J-Bar, they rode directly to the barn. The horses had not been ridden far, but they would appreciate having their cinches loosed, being offered water. Glen glanced unhappily toward the nearest bunkhouse. He found himself hoping that the Fain brothers were not around. He had no

wish to be the bearer of bad news, but he was designated to bring the worst sort of news to the young blond cowboys. He followed Amanda toward the barn, one more riddle passing briefly through his mind:

Who killed Will Fain, and why?

Glen had no answer for that either, and little time to ponder it. As they reached the barn's doors Ben Case stepped forward to meet them. The sleeves of his white shirt were rolled up on his brawny forearms. His face was stony. His eyes watched with unhealthy interest as Amanda dismounted and Glen Strange swung down from his gray horse's back.

'What are you doing here?' Case demanded, striding toward Glen Case, his eyes menacing. 'You're supposed to be out on the south range.'

'I asked Glen to ride in with me,' Amanda said quietly. Her recent confidence seemed to be blunted by the angry manner of the J-Bar foreman. Case could not snap directly back at his

new employer, but he could continue to glower fiercely at Strange. Amanda tried to soothe Case. 'I needed someone to ride to town with me.'

'I would have done it,' Case said without lowering his gaze.

Glen spoke up. 'I had to come in anyway, Case. I met a fellow out there and he wanted me to give you a message.' Case's eyebrows drew together, his lips barely parted as he answered.

'Yeah? What fellow?'

Glen paused, tipped bask his hat and smiled. 'Why, it was old Wichita — you must remember him. He wants you to — '

'Shut up!' Ben Case said, taking another menacing step forward. His eyes flickered to Amanda. It was obvious he did not want her to hear whatever it was that Glen was about to say. The foreman said to him in a low voice, 'I knew it was no coincidence that you rode in when you did. I should have guessed who sent you.' His anger was building so that he was having

trouble forming words. There was a fleck of spittle at the corner of his mouth. He was as furious as Glen had ever seen an man.

'Look, Case — ' he began. That was as far as Strange got. Ben Case uttered a strangled roar deep in his throat and flung himself at Glen Strange. The foreman's body caught Glen solidly in the ribs and he was driven back against his horse. The stolid gray stood still, but Amanda's pale young blue roan reared up, backing away, its hoofs swiping at the air dangerously. Glen saw Amanda draw away from the horse and drop its reins.

Case hadn't waited to begin his brutal assault. He fired two overhand rights in a row at Glen's skull. The first glanced off harmlessly, the second landed above Glen's right eyebrow. He felt blood trickle into his eye, felt his legs wobble slightly. Glen ducked under another blow, slipped under Case's arm and away from the gray horse, bracing himself. Case came on again, but with

the element of surprise gone, he was proven to be less of a fighter. Probably, like many brawlers, he had imagined his first blow taking Strange to his knees. Nothing of the sort had happened, and now the foreman had to figure how to go about fighting a man who was prepared for him.

A woman screamed and yelled. It was not Amanda, Glen thought. It must have been Nora who had cried out, but he did not glance away to confirm that guess. His eyes remained fixed on Ben Case as the foreman, shirt open now, stood bent forward, fists clenched. With a muffled grunt he attacked Glen again. Glen Strange was ready for the huffing, wildly swinging cowboy. He set himself and jabbed two straight lefts into Case's face. Each shot was solid, each rocked Case's head back on its platform. The right-hand shot that Glen followed with arced over Ben Case's guard and landed flush on his cheekbone, splitting the flesh there, and Case staggered backward.

There was no mercy in Glen Strange just then. He couldn't know what might pop into Case's mind in his rage. It could be that, feeling himself beaten, he would grab for his holstered gun to finish matters. Glen stepped forward each time the foreman took a step back, keeping up the pressure, firing both fists with measured effort as Case fought back wildly with looping, ineffective blows. Case's back came up against the wall of the barn and Glen Strange unloaded two more pounding blows, a left which rolled Ben Case's eyes back in his skull and a brutal right hand shot that sent him sliding down the wall of the barn where he remained seated, fists unclenched, blood from his split cheek tracing its way across his face and down across his throat.

Glen stood over him, panting, his eyes still trickling blood. Case's eyes were focused malevolently on Glen Strange.

Glen told him, 'Wichita says he wants his cut.'

Glen saw now that it was indeed Nora who had joined their group. She stood watching Glen, her eyes no less malevolent than Ben Case's, but she said nothing. It was Amanda who spoke next.

'You're fired, Case. Get off the J-Bar.'

'You can't fire him!' Nora shouted with triumph, with mockery. 'You're forgetting the terms of the will. You can't fire him, little lady.' The smile on Nora's face was taunting and cruel.

'No, that's right,' Amanda said. 'All right then — Case, I want you to ride to Cripple Creek. Give the mayor my greetings and ask at the post office if any mail for J-Bar might have been misdirected there.' Case just stared at her dully. He made no attempt to rise. Amanda had another thought.

'After you've done that, I want you to ride to Castle Rock. Give the same message to the mayor there and ask about my mail.'

Glen couldn't help smiling. The ride was one of over a hundred and fifty

miles, round-trip. Ben Case would be gone for quite some time, during which Amanda would have had time to think up more errands for Case to run. One thing was certain. Case might still have a job, but he wasn't going to have much to do with running J-Bar from now on.

'Think he'll go?' Glen asked as they watched Nora help Ben to his feet and lead him toward the house.

'He'll go somewhere off the ranch, and that's all I want.'

Leading their horses, they walked toward the bunkhouse where Tiny stood watching from the steps, hands on his bony hips. Glen had untied his blue bandana and now held it pressed to the cut in his eyebrow. Amanda had offered to help with the wound, but it was obvious to both of them that she wasn't capable in that area. 'Tiny will run a few stitches through it and put a plaster over it,' Glen assured her. A yard man on a cattle ranch was the nearest thing to a doctor a battered cowboy was likely to find, and they got plenty of

practice patching up scrapes, cuts and fractured bones.

Hitching their horses loosely, they ascended the three wooden steps, Tiny frowning as he watched. He glanced at the riding pants Amanda wore and frowned more deeply. It was a rare thing to see a woman in trousers.

'I saw a part of it,' Tiny said to Glen, removing the hand he held to his eye. 'Ben got in at least one good one, huh? What started it, if it's my business?'

'He sort of forgot who was boss around here,' was Glen's brief reply. Tiny shrugged as if it were of no real interest to him.

'Come on in and I'll try stitching you up a little. Let me find my needle and thread and bottle of carbolic.'

Glen winced mentally. Carbolic acid was the cure-all poured into wounds large and small on man and animal alike. It did the job, but it burned like hell even in small amounts.

Amanda leaned against the zinc sink, arms folded, as Glen seated himself in a

wooden chair and Tiny rummaged through his pantry.

'Are the Fain brothers around?' Glen Strange asked.

'Out to the woodpile,' Tiny said. 'Why?'

'I've got some news for them. About their brother.'

'Oh,' Tiny said expressionlessly. He knew from the look on Glen's face that the news was not good. 'Get a grip on that chair, Glen,' Tiny suggested as he threaded the needle. 'Miss Amanda, you might want to turn your head if you're feeling squeamish.'

Amanda watched the first piercing the needle made and then she did turn away, not feeling squeamish exactly, but not wishing to see pain inflicted on a man she was coming to like very much. Peering through the four-paned window of the bunkhouse, she saw movement beyond the oaks. Near the barn three men were grouped together. Earl and Charles Buchanan were in close conversation with Ben Case.

Now what could that be about? All three men looked toward the bunkhouse and Amanda did begin to feel uneasy. They had something in mind, that was certain.

But what!

She was doubly glad that she had forced Glen Strange to return with her to the ranch. She doubted she would feel comfortable without having him around for a long while.

And that, too, was a disturbing thought.

7

'Well, I suppose there's sense to what you say,' Tiny was saying as the three stood around the bunkhouse kitchen drinking coffee. He looked from Amanda to Glen Strange whose bruised and plastered eye gave him a somewhat sinister appearance. They had just finished telling Tiny about the ranch's new policy where it concerned rehiring men who had just gotten caught up in the gold frenzy and were really decent hands. 'You say you're leaving it up to me to choose who stays and who goes?'

'You know the men better than we do,' Amanda said.

'That's so.' Tiny looked doubtful still. 'Of course, Ben won't like this seeing that he's already decided that they should all be fired after turning their backs on the brand.'

'Ben Case has no say in this,'

Amanda said and there was steel in her voice.

Glen told him, 'You don't have to worry about what Ben Case says. He won't be around much from here on out.'

Tiny put his tin coffee cup aside. Pursing his lips, he said quietly, 'I guess I'd better go out and call the Fain brothers over if you're still needing to talk to them.'

'He doesn't like the idea of me taking over,' Amanda said as Tiny clomped down the steps toward the woodpile.

'He just doesn't like change,' Glen said, placing his own cup aside. 'There's been too much of it around here lately.'

'I suppose you're right. Do you want me to stay around while you inform the Fain brothers that Will's been killed?'

'If you like. I can tell them what's happened, as much as I know. But you'll have to be the one to send them back to the south range to relieve Bobby.'

The conversation with the Fains was not an easy one, but both Rod and Austin seemed to have been expecting the worst. Austin said only, 'We'd better get back out there, then.'

'I'm . . . sorry,' Amanda Buchanan told the blond cowboys and they regarded her with uncertain gratitude.

'Thank you, ma'am,' Austin muttered and the two reset their hats and started toward the bunkhouse door. Glen reminded them to take an extra horse along and they nodded and trudged onward.

Tiny had been waiting outside. Now he entered, bringing with him a lanky, sad-eyed cowhand of medium height, hat held in his hands.

'This is Calvin Traylor. He wants to come back to work on the J-Bar. After what you said, Miss Buchanan.'

Amanda looked briefly at the repentant cowboy, glanced at Glen and then asked Tiny, 'Can you work with this man? Is he a troublemaker?'

'He works hard,' Tiny replied. 'Never

caused any trouble around the ranch.'

'Ma'am — ' Calvin Traylor began apologetically, but Amanda interrupted him. She had heard all she needed to know. The J-Bar was desperate for men.

'Get yourself settled,' Amanda said decisively. 'Tiny, when Bobby Trapp comes in, have Calvin help him bury Will Fain. After that, have them go over and relieve those two old gophers who've been guarding the mausoleum.'

Glen smiled at the reference to Buster Haynes and Len Crutcher, but he admired the way Amanda was taking charge of *her* ranch. With that, she was ready to go, but Glen still had questions. He waited until Traylor, saddle roll over his shoulder, had walked back into the bunkroom before he asked them.

'The night that J. Pierce was killed, Tiny?'

'Yes,' the white-haired man responded warily.

'Where was Nora? She had to have heard the commotion if she was in the

big house. No matter how muffled the shots were. Was she there?'

Tiny sighed and his face hardened and then softened again wistfully as if he were struggling with a decision, one long repressed. 'I'll tell you,' he answered at length.

Amanda and Glen waited patiently. The low sun shone through the window of the kitchen. A bluebottle fly pounded its head repetitively against the glass.

'She was visiting her mother.'

'Her mother?' Amanda said. 'I thought — '

Tiny held up a hand for patience. 'She had heard that they were camped down near Honey Bear. Nora wanted to see her.'

'Camped?' Glen said. He was still considering the gypsy looks of Nora, wondering. Tiny cleared matters up immediately.

'Her mother's an Indian. A Paiute.'

'And she abandoned her baby on a white man's doorstep!' Amanda said, shocked by the revelation.

'I had her do it,' Tiny said, and his old eyes faded. 'We were married. Nora is my daughter.'

'I don't understand,' Amanda said, her hands spread. She looked to Glen for clarification.

'Likely,' Glen said, 'the Indians didn't want a white man living among them, didn't want his baby growing up Paiute.'

Tiny's expression confirmed Glen's guess. 'I was young — we were young — I couldn't think of what else to do. We left the baby on J. Pierce's doorstep. I knew he had raised three daughters, and thought he might welcome a girl around the house. Thankfully, he did.'

'The old man never knew where she had come from?'

'No. I never admitted it,' Tiny said with a shamefaced expression. 'I did tell Nora when she was older. I thought she had the right to know. She was determined to find her mother, and one day she did. Now they have some sort of underground telegraph between

them that lets Nora know when her mother's in the area. Her mother's getting older now, too. They get along well enough.'

'But not well enough for Nora to return to her people?' Amanda asked.

'Could you run off and become an Indian, ma'am? It's the same for Nora. It would just be too different, too hard, and besides, she's been well taken care of. She's made her peace with the situation as it is. A long time ago.'

'I see,' Glen said. He had not been distracted by Tiny's tale of woe. He had only wondered why Nora had not heard the uproar that night. Now he knew. He also knew that Nora had not been among J. Pierce's killers. That eased his mind. After all, Amanda was now living under the same roof as Nora.

He did have one more question: 'What about Nora and Ben Case? Is there something between them? You didn't answer me the last time I asked you.'

'I did,' Tiny differed. 'I told you I

134

don't know and it was none of your business. I suppose,' he said more thoughtfully, 'she must have some sort of liking for him. He's not bad looking and she's of that age when young women imagine things. There aren't many what you might call eligible men around here.' He shrugged and fell silent, having convinced Glen that he really did not know if Case and his daughter were romantically involved.

Calvin Traylor had reappeared in the doorway, shifting his feet uncomfortably and they let the conversation break off. 'Just wondered what you wanted me to do,' the young cowhand said.

'Give the man a job, Tiny,' Amanda instructed. 'Mr Strange and I have to be going now.' To Glen she said, 'We'll already be lucky if we make it to town before nightfall.'

Riding out, they crossed the grasslands and started up the trail through the thin pine forest where the air was cool and heavy with the scent of the tall trees. They passed two men who were

seated on the ground, each of them wearing a part of a cavalry soldier's uniform. These two raised weary eyes to them, but otherwise made no move.

At the crest of the trail before the path again started down toward the spreading acreage of the south range, they met Bobby Trapp. The cowboy was leading a small pinto horse weighted down with a blanket-wrapped burden. Glen and Amanda halted their horses and waited for him to reach them.

Bobby looked at Glen's black eye and commented dryly, 'Well, it looks like you've been having fun. What happened?'

'Just a little disagreement with Ben Case,' Glen said casually. Bobby looked as if he had something to say, and so Glen drew his gray horse nearer. 'What is it, Bobby?'

'I've been thinking, Glen.' Bobby glanced back at the bundle on the pinto horse's back. 'Things aren't getting any better around here, are they?'

'Not so's you'd notice it,' Glen had to admit.

'Remember when I suggested that we just pull out of here? Have you given that any more thought, Glen. I mean before someone takes us home wrapped in our blankets.'

'I've thought of it,' Glen answered. 'But how can we? I couldn't ride off now and leave the woman to her bad luck.'

Bobby looked toward Amanda, her neat little body and erect back, her blonde hair shimmering in the sunlight filtering through the pines. 'No,' Bobby said finally, 'I guess you couldn't.' The way he said it indicated that he, himself, wouldn't mind leaving the J-Bar.

'Bobby,' Glen said, putting a hand on Bobby Trap's wrist. 'We've always stuck together — through everything. Stick with it for a while longer, won't you?'

It was a long minute before Bobby nodded and said with some regret, 'Sure, Glen. I'll stick with you.'

When Bobby had gone, Glen and Amanda started on their way again. Below, they could now see the cattle scattered across the miles of long grass. Amanda said, 'There's no need to stop and see the Fain brothers, is there?'

'No,' Glen replied, having no wish to visit the grieving brothers himself. 'As you said, we're liable to run out of daylight as it is.'

The town of Big Springs didn't seem much more welcoming in the hazy glow of purple dusk than it had in full daylight. The same long row of rickety structures along the main street, the same loafers or others like them gathered in front of the noisy saloons. Amanda had been hoping to reach town earlier and possibly even have the time to return to J-Bar before dark. Now it was obvious that they would have to spend the night in Big Springs. They weren't willing to risk a night ride through the gantlet of frustrated fortune hunters and thieves.

'There's still a light on in Craig Dumont's office,' Amanda said, indicating a yellow-brick building set off the main street. 'Good. It's time this business about my brothers' inheritance was cleared up.'

'Do you want me to go with you?' Glen asked.

'No.' Amanda shook her head worriedly. 'I think he'll be more willing to talk to me if I'm alone.' She looked skyward to where the first stars were already beginning to shimmer. 'You'd better go over to the hotel and get two rooms for us.'

'All right,' Glen said a little doubtfully. He didn't like leaving Amanda alone even though she should be safe enough in the heart of town, even as rough as it was.

He sat his gray horse, stroking its heated neck, watching until Amanda had swung down in front of the lawyer's office, knocked on the door and been admitted.

'Let's go,' he murmured to the horse.

'I'll find us all a place to spend the night.'

The desk clerk, young and energetic, possibly trying to make a good impression in the early days of employment, cheerfully took Glen's reservations although Strange was the only trail-dusty man to be seen among the hotel patrons.

Walking out onto the porch, which was illuminated by the light spilling out from inside the hotel, he stood for a moment, thumbs hooked in his belt, looking down the noisy, crowded street. Big Springs had an electric feel about it. It was pretty much the same as the excitement in a gold-rush town, he thought. A lot of men poised to get rich, wasting what little they had on whiskey and gambling.

Glen thought idly how ironic it was that everyone despised the wealthy and yet every man was out there hoping to become one himself, whether it was with stolen gold or on a lucky spin of the roulette wheel.

Shrugging conjecture aside, he stepped

off the porch and swung heavily into leather, walking the gray along a side street, searching for a stable. There he requested that his horse be grained and curried, and reserved a stall for Amanda's horse which he would bring over later. That settled, he walked out onto the main street again, studying the unfocused bustle from the shadows of a general store awning.

He still could feel the excitement. A sort of manic energy that had to be dispersed with whiskey, in brawls, loud boasting and breakage. It made no sense at all. None of it. He wandered away from the center of town, asking his way toward the sheriff's office, a red-brick building with bars on the windows and a feeble light showing in one window. He already knew that Sheriff Fowler had left for Arizona Territory to visit relatives, knew that his deputies had gone out toward the J-Bar and surrounding lands, supposedly to keep a lid on the activities of the looters. He had met both of the

deputies: Ward, the fat one who had been riding with the scavengers, and Po Hilgers who would not be coming back.

Someone, however, was manning the sheriff's office and so Glen stepped up onto the porch and rapped at the door. Finding it open a crack, he went in to the clean, dimly lit interior.

'Sheriff ain't here,' a voice crackled.

'I know that.'

'Deputies neither.'

'I know,' Glen said without emphasis.

The speaker was a woman of middle years, her long salt-and-pepper hair straggling out from beneath a red bandana. She was stout, firm looking. She had a mop in her hand, bucket at her feet and a challenging look in her brown eyes.

'Well, what do you want then?'

Glen removed his hat. 'I was hoping to come by some information,' he said, but the woman snapped:

'If you're wanting to know the way to the J-Bar ranch — '

Glen held up a hand and smiled.

'No, ma'am. I work on the J-Bar.'

'Because,' she continued as if he hadn't spoken, 'if I meet one more of these crazy men running all around the country looking for buried treasure — what's the matter with men, mister?'

'I wouldn't know. Anyway, I'm just a friend of the family, and I — '

'What family! Ain't no family unless you count . . . ' her eyes grew sly. 'You're talking about the girl, aren't you? That pretty blonde? I seen her.'

'Her name's Amanda Buchanan,' Glen told the woman. 'J. Pierce's granddaughter. But she's not the reason I dropped by, either. I was hoping that the sheriff might be back sometime soon.'

'He might; he might not. People think that he ran off because of all the trouble. Marston Fowler never ran from trouble in his life! How was he to know how crazy things would get?' she asked challengingly. 'He hadn't seen his sister in twelve years and he'd been planning that trip to Tucson for nearly six

months. He wasn't going to cancel it because a few crazy men came into the county and started digging things up. No sir,' she said definitely. 'My husband is the best lawman this county ever had.'

'I believe you,' Glen said. 'Mrs Fowler,' he went on, now having a name to go with the cleaning woman, 'I didn't come by to criticize the sheriff either.' Again she continued as if he had not spoken to her.

'Someone's got to keep the office clean in his absence. That falls to me, of course. Lazy Po Hilgers and that Abel Ward — they're the ones who are hiding out from the trouble around here. No-good deputies, and if I have anything to say about it they won't have a job when Marston gets back.'

Glen was just a little tired of the woman's complaining. He tried to get the conversation back on track. She helped him in that direction by saying, 'Well, you've told me everything you are not and all that you don't want.

Why is it you did stop in here, mister?'

'I was hoping to find out something about a man named Wichita. I know he's got an outlaw past. I wondered if he was still a wanted man.'

'I never heard Marston mention the name,' the sheriff's wife said. She had placed her mop and bucket aside and now leaned against the sheriff's desk, arms folded.

'Is there a file of Wanted posters around?' Glen said, glancing at the half-dozen notices pinned to the wall behind the woman's back.

'I wouldn't know about that,' she said without courtesy. 'I don't dig through Marston's office.'

'What about Ben Case,' Glen tried, and he saw Mrs Fowler's expression alter slightly.

'What about him?'

'It's said that he, too, has a shadowy past. I wondered if his name had ever been cleared.'

'Ben Case, if that's what you choose to call him, has been here for seven

years and never caused a moment's trouble,' she said a little defensively.

'He's not using his own name?'

'I didn't say that,' the woman answered, although she had implied that.

'It doesn't matter, I don't suppose,' Glen said, trying a smile on the sheriff's wife. 'I was just wondering. With all this trouble, I kind of took it upon myself to watch out for Amanda Buchanan.'

'I'll bet you did,' Fowler's wife said, her eyes narrowing knowingly.

'If you can't tell me anything,' Glen said, putting his hat on, 'I'll apologize for wasting your time.'

She nodded, straightened and touched her face nervously. Finally, as if it were a struggle to speak, she told Glen Strange, 'The sheriff should be back tomorrow or the day after. I'd let him handle any trouble that you might be having.'

'I hope he can,' Glen said, and with a nod he departed, emerging again onto the street where the noise from the saloons cascaded toward him. Glen

reflected that he had learned nothing, solved nothing. But then he had expected little.

Gloomily, he tramped toward the hotel, noticing as he passed that Craig Dumont's office was now closed and dark. He brightened a little at that. Amanda was finished with her business. He would clean up a little and take her to dinner.

Along the boardwalk Glen shouldered past noisy, half-drunk men. He could recall times past when he had enjoyed spending an evening in the saloon, drinking beer with his friends, re-telling the old stories. Maybe all of the merriment could only be appreciated from the inside. Now these men seemed dirty and crude and vaguely threatening. Maybe, he was forced to reflect, he had just grown too old for that sort of pleasure.

The same diffident clerk was on duty when Glen returned to the brightly lit white interior of the hotel. Glen walked past him, boot-heels clicking against the

polished floor. He drew a few looks from handsomely dressed men and brightly clad women. Paying them no mind, he went upstairs and tapped on the door of Amanda's room.

There was no answer. He tried again and then another time. Frowning, he returned to the desk and asked the clerk, 'Miss Amanda Buchanan, has she come in?'

'Are you Mr Strange? Miss Buchanan sent word that she had gone out and would see you in the morning.'

'Did she say where she was going?' Glen asked in puzzlement. Where *would* she go?

'No, sir, that was all of the message. A young man brought word.'

'All right,' Glen growled. He went out onto the porch again. It was fully dark now and the saloons seemed to be gathering momentum. Someone uptown fired a gun into the air. Where was Amanda? There was no point in looking for her, having no clue where to begin. Perhaps Amanda and Dumont

had decided to go to dinner together. That seemed the most obvious possibility.

Glen had no other guesses and so he temporarily abandoned thoughts of chivalry and started across the street toward a small restaurant there. His complaining stomach was one thing he could do something about.

The ceiling was low, the tables made of long planks. There were a dozen or so men eating, and Glen took a seat, lifting a finger to the harried waitress in the stained dress. There would be no menu, he knew. Just a plate of whatever was available. Glen watched the waitress weave her way through the knot of patrons, closed his eyes briefly and then opened them again as he heard someone slide onto the bench opposite him. When he looked up it was directly into the eyes of the man called Wichita.

'You get around,' Wichita said without expression. His sidekick was beside

him. In this better light Glen could see that the short, dark man had one ear missing.

'So do you,' Glen commented. Wichita leaned forward, bony hands clenched together.

'Did you give Ben Case my message?'

'I did.'

'What was his reply?'

'This,' Glen said, touching his split eyebrow. Wichita's thin lips twitched in what might have been amusement. 'He seemed to have the idea that I was on your side.'

'Perhaps you are,' Wichita said. 'Perhaps you will be before this is all over.'

'I don't think — '

'If you want my help finding the blonde girl.'

8

Glen Strange's face carried an ugly glare. The waitress had returned with a plate of food, but he edged it aside with his elbow, his eyes coldly fixed on Wichita.

'What do you know about Amanda?' he asked quietly.

'Quite a bit,' the gunman said. 'As you've said, I get around.'

'If you've snatched her — '

Wichita was wagging his head. 'Not me, cowboy, but I know what happened to her.'

'Do you want to tell me,' Glen said, 'or are we going to have trouble? You know I've got my Colt aimed your way under the table.'

'Yes,' Wichita drawled, 'I know it. But you won't need it. I'm here for honest dealing. I'll show you where the girl is in exchange for your help

with my problem.'

'Your problem would be?'

'Ben Case.'

'Of course,' Glen nodded. 'So he doesn't wish to talk to you.'

'No. And with good reason. We saw him riding this way earlier, and I was of half a mind to have it out with Mr Case then and there but, you see, he had two other men riding with him and it would have been more of a fight than Toby and I were ready for. Somebody would have been killed, and right now I need Case alive. I wouldn't mind staying that way myself,' he added thinly.

'You say that Case had two other men with him? Were they dressed like dudes?' Glen asked.

'As a matter of fact, they were,' Wichita said. 'Do you know them?'

Earl and Charles Buchanan. It had to be. So the three of them had found common cause. Well, it figured, Glen thought. Amanda had taken all the chips in the game so far, and they were all resentful.

'What do you figure Case owes you for?' Glen Strange asked. He slid his revolver back into its holster and noticed that Toby, Wichita's dark, silent companion made a somewhat similar movement under the table.

'I figure he owes me for seven years in Yuma prison,' Wichita said. 'It's a long story, longer than you need to hear, but there was a dust-up down Socorro way seven years ago. A bank job that went wrong. Case was involved. I wasn't, but I took the fall for it.'

'Why?'

'I was young enough to believe outlaws had a code of honor. I didn't figure on doing seven years, but that's what I got. Ben wrote me that he was onto a good thing out west. Running a ranch for an old man who couldn't last long. When the old man was gone, Ben told me, he'd share the ranch with me. That promise was enough to keep me silent, knowing that in the end I'd have a good life to show for my time served.'

'I suppose Ben Case decided that he didn't owe you after awhile.'

'I never heard a word from him the last five years. I came by to ask him about affairs. I hear the old man died.'

'He did,' Glen answered. He didn't think it was in his best interests to tell Wichita that Ben Case had profited nothing from J. Pierce's death. He did say, 'Murdered in his bed.'

'Ben must've got tired of waiting,' Toby commented. It was the first time Glen had heard the little man speak.

'So have I gotten tired!' Wichita said, showing his frustration. 'The man owes me something for my time.'

All of this conversation was beside the point. Glen wouldn't have minded hearing the whole story another time, but his concern now was only with Amanda's safety.

'You say you know something about Miss Buchanan. What happened, Wichita?'

Amanda Buchanan was shown into Craig Dumont's office and seated in a

154

tasteful white chair with a red velvet-cushioned seat and back. It matched nothing else in what was otherwise a man's decor with heavy oak furniture, low-beamed and sterile with a glass-front bookcase holding legal volumes. The room smelled faintly of aromatic pipe tobacco, though no pipes were in evidence. Dumont wore an expression of concern and weariness as he sagged into his chair facing Amanda and propped one elbow on his desk, leaning forward to study her.

'Is there some problem, Miss Buchanan?' the lawyer asked. He had begun inadvertently fingering the spider-shaped scar on his gaunt cheek.

'It concerns the status of my brothers' inheritance — ' Amanda began, but Dumont immediately halted her with two raised palms.

'I have told you all I can about that,' he insisted.

'Yes,' Amanda said, rushing her words, 'but you have to understand. Charles and Earl are making life

miserable out at the J-Bar, slinking around at night, shooting accusing glances at me, prying into — '

'I have told you — and them — all that I am allowed to under the dictates of the will,' Dumont said, taking a deep slow breath to calm himself. Your grandfather's terms are quite clear.'

'Why would they be forced to remain here? For three weeks! What can possibly change in three weeks?'

'The will is quite specific, Miss Buchanan. Perhaps you — they — and I might wish to finish this all as soon as possible, but I can do nothing. My hands are tied. You see — ' he said, leaning back more comfortably in his chair, but he was not allowed to finish his sentence.

The cracking sound brought Amanda's head around. Boots could be heard stamping across the floor of the outer office and the three men burst into the room. Charles looked determined but shaken. Earl Buchanan glowered. He was clenching a pistol. Ben Case looked

156

positively wild-eyed and savage. He said nothing but strode to where Dumont sat and placed the muzzle of his Colt revolver against the attorney's neck.

'You two having a nice talk, are you?' he said in a wolfish voice.

'If this is about the will, gentlemen,' Dumont said, managing to retain some control of his emotions.

'That's what it's about,' Earl Buchanan said. He glanced at his sister with distaste. 'Amanda here, the favored child, has got everything from the will. While we are stranded in what might as well be a foreign land, virtually penniless. This is the end of it, Dumont. We want our money.'

'Fifty thousand,' Charles said as if he felt obliged to pitch in. He glanced nervously at his sister and then looked quickly away. He obviously had been dragged into this by his more impetuous, more violent older brother.

'Your grandfather has certainly not left you penniless, gentlemen. None of you,' he added, looking directly into

Ben Case's eyes, but not holding the gaze for long, as Case hovered menacingly over him.

'Yeah,' Case growled, 'I got a job working for someone who won't even let me do my work.'

Amanda studied Ben Case, listened to him. Any veneer of courtesy that he might have exhibited previously had fallen away. He was a savage presence in the little room. She had seen that side of him once before, when he had assaulted Glen Strange, but this was more revealing. The man was a thug, pure and simple. She wondered idly if the reason Ben Case clung to his job had something to do with the profit to be made from it. She had seen the ranch ledgers, and it was obvious to her that the sales of J-Bar cattle had diminished year by year although they should have increased.

Grandfather, at ninety, had surely not been riding the range often enough to see all that might have been going on there. He had trusted Ben Case, and it

had finally come to this.

Earl Buchanan tried to assume leadership and turn the conversation to a more reasonable level. 'Look here, Dumont, we understand that you have an obligation as executor, but J. Pierce is dead. What can it matter to him if we are given what is rightfully ours now?'

'Right now,' Charles put in, but it emerged from his throat more as a chirp than a threat.

'No more talking,' Ben Case said roughly. Now he drew back the hammer of his revolver. 'Come across with that fifty thousand now or pay the price.'

'Stop it!' Amanda said, but no one so much as glanced at her.

'Killing him won't do it,' Earl Buchanan said, again apparently trying to keep Case in check. 'We might never find it if he's dead.'

'Then we'll beat it out of him!' Case vowed. The man was on the brink of mad violence. Now Case did turn his eyes to Amanda as he nudged Dumont

harder with the barrel of his pistol. 'Or out of her while he watches.'

'Not my sister,' Charles said, but the small man didn't appear to be that shocked by the suggestion.

'Calm down, Case,' Earl said, drawing a nasty scowl from the ranch foreman. 'We'll get him to talk, but not here. People do pass by and Glen Strange is liable to come looking for Amanda.'

'You're right,' Ben Case was forced to admit. 'Where, then?'

'It's your town.'

Case was briefly thoughtful, then he nodded his head decisively, 'I know the place,' he said. He let his eyes linger barbarously on Amanda. 'You'll be sorry you ever tried to ride roughshod over Ben Case, lady.'

Amanda tried to reply, but found her throat constricted. She had never thought of herself as a timorous female, but these men, in this situation, were utterly intimidating. And probably quite deadly.

She was helped roughly to her feet by her brothers, neither of whom would meet her gaze,

Charles puffing with the minor exertion. Amanda demanded of her younger brother, 'Why are you in league with this man?'

'We all have something to gain, and everything to lose if we take no action.'

Amanda believed that she understood then. Her brothers had the fifty thousand dollars to gain. Ben Case would have the J-Bar if she were out of the way. Her brothers may not have intended for it to fall out this way, but she felt certain now that Case meant to kill her for the property. He would have made some sort of arrangement with Earl and Charles that he was to get the J-Bar in which they had no interest if he helped them obtain the fifty thousand. She knew that for a certainty. And she knew by the way her brothers' eyes shifted away from her that they had no objections to removing her so long as they got what they wanted. It was

painful to realize that her own blood relatives viewed her only as a commodity to be traded for gold. She . . .

Suddenly there was a scuffle in the room. She saw Craig Dumont reach for his desk drawer, saw Ben Case leap that way. Case's pistol barrel cracked against Dumont's skull and the lawyer, still reaching for the gun hidden in his desk sagged to the floor, blood seeping from his scalp.

Amanda heard a scream hanging in the air, realized it was her own.

'Shut her up!' Case yelled frantically. Hatless now, his dark hair hung in his eyes.

'You might have killed him,' Charles said, staring at the collapsed lawyer.

'The bastard was going for a gun,' Case said sarcastically, 'what would you have me do?'

'We've got to get out of here,' Earl said calmly. 'Someone may have heard the scream.'

'Get up!' Case hollered at Dumont who was trying but failing to do just

that. Grasping the edge of his desk with one hand, he was unable to get his legs under him. 'Hell, we'll have to carry him,' Case said with disgust.

'Wait a minute,' Earl said. He had been examining the pictures hanging on the walls. Now he swung a hinged portrait of President Grant aside, revealing a wall safe. 'Maybe we don't have to worry about taking him anywhere. Open this safe, Dumont!' Earl Buchanan ordered.

In a daze Dumont was hoisted to his feet by Case and Charles and led limp-legged to the small round safe in the wall.

They held him braced before the safe. The lawyer's head lolled on his neck. Ben Case slapped him twice, hard, but they got no reaction from Dumont.

'You hit him too hard,' Earl Buchanan said. 'He's out on his feet. Now what?'

'Shut up,' Ben Case growled. He had assumed command again. 'We'll get the

combination out of him and come back later. It'll be easier that way anyhow.'

The plan, quickly formulated, called for the three men to take Dumont and Amanda to a disused hay barn nearby. Close enough to town, it was still set apart enough for them to use whatever tactics might be needed on their captives without interruption.

Amanda was taken roughly by her arm. Ben Case escorted her to the doorway, his pocked face set in a twisted grimace. Earl and Charles led the wobbly Craig Dumont out of the door after a cautious inspection of the alleyway. There were occasional shadowy figures passing the head of the alley, but none interested in their business. Each passing silhouette caught Amanda's eye, sparking hope.

Where was Glen Strange!

These three armed men might prove to be too much for Glen to tackle, but she had no doubt that he would attempt whatever was necessary for her safety. Why had she come to Dumont's

office alone? She thought that if she ever managed to escape she would go nowhere without Glen's quiet strength beside her.

'Let's keep moving,' Ben Case growled. There were too many eyes here for his liking, and the three started down the alley toward the dark and empty land beyond the town limits.

But they had been seen. Not by Glen Strange, but by Wichita and Toby who had followed the group of men into Big Springs. Wichita was determined to have his facedown with Ben Case no matter what it took. The man owed him recompense for seven years of his life. Yet it was still three guns against their two, and Toby, if loyal, could also prove erratic. It therefore made sense to track down Glen Strange in the restaurant and enlist his gun in their cause. The cowboy would walk through hell for Amanda, Wichita knew. He, himself, could not care less about the woman, but that was no matter, so long as the three had a common goal.

* * *

'Where is she?' Glen Strange now demanded in the restaurant. He was already on his feet, any thought of eating his supper vanished. A rage hot enough to destroy a simple urge like hunger had risen in his chest. Case, greedy and unstable, was liable to do anything, Glen knew, but that Amanda's two brothers would assault her was despicable. What sort of Southern gentlemen had these two become?

'Let's talk outside,' Wichita said, noticing that the men around them had their eyes fixed now on the furious Glen Strange. Glen nodded and was escorted out into the cool of the evening.

'Where?' he demanded again once they were out on the restaurant porch.

'There's an old building south of town. Looks like it used to be some sort of warehouse, maybe a hay barn. They were leading their two prisoners directly there when we last saw them.'

'Let's go then,' Glen Strange said.

'We need some sort of plan,' Wichita argued, taking Glen's arm. Glen shook the hand off angrily.

'Then think one up along the way,' he said, I'm not leaving Amanda in their clutches for a minute longer than I have to.'

Wichita's mouth tightened and he shrugged helplessly. Fine, now he had enlisted another hothead, a man as erratic and unthinking as he knew Toby to be. Wichita himself was in no particular hurry. He was more interested in the results than in quick action. So long as he and Ben Case remained alive he could not care less about the outcome of tonight's encounter. He took Strange briefly by the arm again and said as much.

'I want Case alive.'

'I won't kill him,' Glen promised. 'Unless he's done something that makes it necessary.'

That wasn't much of an agreement, but Wichita knew he had no choice now. Hoping that Glen could show

167

some restraint, he followed along, Toby in tow, as Glen crossed the street and entered the alley fronting the lawyer's office. There was no one to be seen along its length. Nothing moved in the night except the three stalking men.

Yet something ugly hovered there. Something dark and quite ominous, promising violence.

* * *

Earl and Ben Case stood over Craig Dumont. The lawyer was sagged against the wall in the corner of the hay barn where the scent of rot was strong despite the open door which allowed the chill air of evening to drift wisps of hay across the empty floor of the sagging building.

'You are going to talk, Dumont,' Ben Case said, his voice throttled with anger, and he shook Dumont so violently that the attorney's head rattled against the wooden wall. Earl Buchanan put a restraining hand on Case's

shoulder, which caused the man with the pocked face to whirl toward him angrily.

'Keep your hands off me,' Case said in a warning voice and the Southerner drew back half a step.

'Dead men can't talk, Case,' Earl said calmly. 'You've got to go easy on him.'

'He's not hurt that bad,' Case replied, although there was a hint of doubt in his tone.

'You shouldn't have roughed him up,' Charles Buchanan piped up, but neither of the other men paid any attention to him.

Amanda sat against the face of a partition not far distant. Charles had been assigned to watch her, but now his attention was diverted as well. Discovering where the fifty thousand dollars was hidden was far more important than anything Amanda could do or say. She wondered briefly if she could make a dash for the door, run into the night calling for help. Would they shoot her down? Or simply tackle her before she

could go ten feet?

Probably the latter, she thought, as Charles, remembering his assignment, edged back toward his sister. Even now he could not let his gaze meet hers. 'What did I ever do to you?' she asked in a whisper and she saw Charles flinch slightly. He did not answer.

'What do you think we ought to do?' Ben Case asked roughly as Craig Dumont continued to show no signs of responding. Earl Buchanan shrugged.

'He's bound to come around sooner or later. I don't think moving him is a good idea. Suppose we just wait and watch?'

'He could be faking it,' Ben Case said, crouching down in front of the battered Dumont. Blood had trickled across his forehead and over one eye, hardening to a purplish crust. There was a large lump on his temple where Case had pistol-whipped him. His body was inert. Although his eyes did open from time to time, they were utterly unfocused. Case's angry zeal

had retarded their function. If Dumont were alert they could continue with their plan — to threaten Amanda with injury if Dumont refused to surrender the gold. But you cannot threaten an unconscious man and so the three stood around aimlessly, the interior of the barn lighted only by a low-burning lantern hanging on a nail on the wall beside them. Nothing was going according to plan.

'What if he dies?' Charles Buchanan asked uneasily.

'He's not going to die,' Case snapped in frustration. 'I didn't hit him that hard.'

'Sometimes it doesn't take much,' Charles observed unhappily. It had gotten to the point where Charles no longer cared so much about the money. True, their business in Mississippi was not doing well, but he longed for the languid South, the warmer weather, the familiar surroundings, friends. He looked again at Amanda and his

heart shrank just a little. It was true.

The girl had done nothing to deserve this.

And how far would the others go? If, for instance, Craig Dumont did not recover, Amanda would be a witness to his murder. What, then, would Earl and this wild-eyed Colorado cowboy do to her?

Yes, Charles reflected as he stood, painted by the shifting shadows cast by the lantern, it was a fool who pursued gold when the price became blood. Given the choice, he thought, he would have thrown down the gun in his hand and walked away from the tangled situation, but when his eyes met those of Ben Case or Earl, he knew that he was mired in this just as deeply as they were. No one was going to let him walk away, and he began to feel that he was becoming as much a prisoner of events as Amanda was.

Amanda heard the wind whispering beyond the building. It was the wind,

was it not? She glanced anxiously that way, recognizing the sounds now — boot leather gliding over the earth. She barely dared hope . . .

9

'This can't continue much longer,' Charles was saying as his brother and Ben Case continued to hover over Craig Dumont pointlessly.

'You're right!' a strange voice boomed from the open door. 'It's already over. Toss down your guns, men.'

Charles Buchanan spun in confusion toward the door where Wichita held his pistol leveled at the three of them. Beside him was Glen Strange, equally ready to shoot, and a small dark man with one ear missing. Charles didn't hesitate; he flung his hands high. The gun dropped from his grip as if it were red-hot. Earl and Ben Case were not so compliant.

'Wichita!' Case yelled in anger, distress and disbelief. Then he swung his pistol violently to the side, smashing the glass chimney of the lantern on the

wall, extinguishing the flame, plunging the hay barn into darkness. Three shots, four, sounded in the close confines of the building, stabbing red-yellow flame. Amanda threw herself flat on the ground, heard a man cry out in pain and prayed that now Glen had come he had not been lured into a death trap.

Men scurried aside behind her, in front of her. Two more gunshots sounded, one near at hand, the other sending a bullet ricocheting off a bit of metal far across the barn. Then silence fell. Complete and utter silence in the black of the night. A man moved, his motion making no more noise that a rat's scuttling, but a pistol shot roared out. Another gun answered, aimed at the muzzle flash of the first and then the barn fell silent again, the acrid scent of gunpowder filling Amanda's nostrils.

She wanted to cry out to Glen, to discover if he was unhurt, to let him know that she was all right, that she had been praying for his arrival. She knew better than to speak as the shadows

continued to move wraithlike around in the darkness, as men searched for cover or tried to find a position from which to attack.

She did not dare move. No one could be sure of his target in the gloom. All she could do was wait and hope. There was a sudden movement at the far end of the barn and a cracking sound as if a boot had struck wood, and in the same moment a patch of deep violet opened in the blackness. A single star appeared and then a man's silhouette covered it as someone rushed out of the open door. Three shots, and then a fourth, followed the ducking figure, but they all must have missed. There was no cry of pain, no shout of anger.

The silence descended again. No second man made a move toward the open side door, but after a minute Amanda heard the sounds of a horse being ridden away at a hard gallop.

Glen Strange cursed silently. He could see no more in the darkness than Amanda could. But someone had

known where a side door was located, taken the chance and kicked it open. Glen had taken one shot at the man, but it was an off-hand shot at an unexpected running target, and he was sure that he had missed. Wichita, standing just above Glen as he crouched against the barn floor, had banged two shots in that direction and Tony, belatedly, had followed with another. None of them tagged flesh. Moments later they, too, heard the sounds of a running horse.

'Who was it?' Wichita hissed. 'Was it Case?'

Glen had no answer for him. The dark silhouette could have been any of the three men they had pursued, although it seemed unlikely that the meek Charles Buchanan would have risked the dash for freedom except out of blind panic.

'Case!' Wichita hollered at the darkness, and then again, 'Case!' But there was no answer from the dark interior of the hay barn. Glen expected someone

to aim and fire at the sound of Wichita's voice, but the silence held. At his side Toby whispered with some anxiousness.

'What now?'

It was a good question, one for which Glen had no answer. Yet he had not forgotten why he had come to this isolated building. His first concern was Amanda's safety and touching Wichita's knee to warn him of his intent, Glen went to his belly against the cold hard floor of the hay barn and tried whispering to her:

'Amanda? Can you hear me. Can you move?'

Now someone did fire in the direction of his voice, but flat against the ground, the bullet whipped overhead and sang off into the night. Toby, now lying prone as well, cut loose with three rapid answering rounds, apparently tagging nothing. When the echo of the shots fell away there was nothing again but silent darkness. The enemy, it seemed, had bunkered down in a secure position from which he refused to be

dislodged. And there was nothing they could do about it.

Wichita wanted to withdraw. Getting cautiously to his feet, he told Glen, 'That was Case who got away, I know it. I'm going to track him. The rest of this is your business, not mine.'

He had eased back toward the door, a reluctant Toby following, when the horseman burst past the entrance to the barn. A dark horse being ridden at a dead run showed itself and the man riding it shot beneath its neck, Indian-style, spraying the front of the hay barn with lead. Toby howled in pain, Wichita fell to one side, firing back wildly with his Colt until the hammer fell on an empty chamber. Pounding feet caught Glen Strange's attention too late. During the brief battle, the other two men had made their dash for the small door at the back of the barn. The second one was just vanishing around the corner into the night as Glen wheeled toward him. There was no chance of getting off a telling shot.

'Bastard!' Glen heard Wichita howl, for there was no doubt that the rider had been Case. 'Let's go, Toby!'

Toby followed faithfully as Wichita ran from the barn, fired one shot from his reloaded pistol skyward out of blind fury, and sprinted toward town. The one-eared man, Glen saw, had been nicked in the leg, for he gimped along resolutely, clutching his thigh with his left hand. The rustling sound near at hand drew Glen's attention. Amanda had gotten to her feet and now she rushed to him, throwing her arms around him.

'They're gone,' she said as she drew back, looking up into his shadowed eyes.

'For now. Let's get you out of here. How's Dumont?'

'I don't know. He's like the walking dead.'

'Is there a doctor in this town?' Glen asked before he realized that Amanda had been here no longer than he himself. 'Let's get him back to his office.'

'That's the first place they'll look,' she objected, 'if they come back.'

'Give me another suggestion,' Glen said, but Amanda could only shake her head. The hotel was too far away; dragging him uptown through the gathered drinking mob would prove too much of a trial.

Amanda clung to Glen for a minute, her fingers clutching his arms tightly. Gradually that grip loosened. She took a slow breath, wiped her hair from her eyes and said, 'Let's get him over to his office.'

It wasn't far, but the unresponsive Dumont still had to be half-carried and they made their way like drunken sailors back to the alley and toward Dumont's office, the attorney reeling between them, now and then muttering something unintelligible past the burbling saliva on his lips.

'Find a lamp,' Glen instructed as they reached the door which stood open, for the lamps inside had been extinguished or had run out of fuel. After a few

fumbling moments, Amanda struck flame to the wick of a standing lamp in Dumont's office and by its wavering illumination Glen shouldered the injured man along and placed him down on the leather sofa there. For a moment he sagged against the wall, staring at the battered face of the lawyer. Then he straightened himself and said, 'This man needs more help than we can give him.'

Amanda nodded. Dumont seemed closer to the grave than recovery. 'We have to find a doctor.'

They did not want to leave Dumont alone, nor did Glen wish to let Amanda out of his sight. The problem was solved by the sudden appearance of Mrs Fowler in the doorway, her scarf and dust apron now removed.

'What's all the racket over here!' the sheriff's wife wanted to know. 'I thought I heard a gunfight out back, too. What's going on?' She put her fingers to her cheeks as she caught sight of the wounded man and said,

'Oh, my God, Mr Dumont! What's been happening here?'

'We'll fill you in later,' Glen promised. 'Just now we need a doctor. Is there one in town?'

'Yes. A young man, Dr Chambliss. He's just arrived, actually, but . . . but, oh, yes, I'll get the doctor.'

They waited in the silent near-darkness of the room for nearly half an hour. Glen removed Dumont's boots and loosened his belt and tie while Amanda did what she could to arrange her hair and clean the smudges of dirt from her face.

Eventually Mrs Fowler returned with a thin, bespectacled young man carrying a black leather bag that showed little signs of use. One corner of his coat collar was turned up, his shirt misbuttoned. After a brief examination, the doctor rose and said, 'Heavily concussed, of course. Not much we can do but wait.'

That was hardly satisfying as a diagnosis, but what else had they

expected? The young man cleaned the blood from Dumont's face and applied peroxide to the split scalp. His stitching was neater than Tiny's, a row of exact little Xs across the lump on Dumont's shaved temple, but he had done little more than could have been accomplished without him. Before returning to his bed, Chambliss did offer the bleak prognosis: 'It could still kill him. If the swelling on his brain gets worse.' Meaning that the doctor had already done all he could do, all anyone could do, and there was a good chance that Ben Case's impulsive pistol whipping might bring a murder charge down on his head.

'I wouldn't try moving him just now,' the doctor added unnecessarily. Then with a shake of his head, the thin man went out into the night, closing the door quietly behind him.

'What will we do with Mr Dumont? I can't stay here all night,' Mrs Fowler said peevishly.

'No,' Amanda replied. 'You've done

enough. I'll sit with him.'

'I don't want you here alone,' Glen said. 'The three of them might decide to circle back. They won't give up on the gold so easily.'

He was wishing that he had talked Amanda into bringing Bobby Trapp to town with them, because he did not feel that he could remain there with her to watch over Dumont. He told her so. 'I've got to track them down, Amanda'

'You don't know where to look.'

'Case will head for the J-Bar or near it. He knows every inch of that land. Wichita doesn't, and Ben will try to lose him there.'

'You don't know that country either,' Amanda pointed out.

Mrs Fowler, who had not yet left, said, 'If my husband was here we could raise a posse in no time.'

But he was not. Case and the Buchanan brothers had to be tracked down, and there was only one man to do it. And if it had to be done, he wanted it done in the open spaces, not

anywhere near Amanda Buchanan. The expression in Amanda's wide blue eyes revealed her own unhappy understanding of the situation.

Bravely she said, 'Do what has to be done, Glen. I'll be all right here, really.'

Glen hesitated then nodded decisively. He walked to Dumont's desk, leaned over and picked up the lawyer's pistol, the one the man had been reaching for when Case beat him down. Wiping it clean on his shirttail, he checked the loads and handed the big Colt to Amanda. She took it tentatively and he asked.

'You do know how to use this, don't you?' he asked.

'Cock, point and fire. Repeat if necessary,' Amanda said, attempting a smile. Her lips only twitched, but it was a pretty, somehow brave expression. Glen leaned to her and kissed her gently.

'I'll lock the door on my way out. You should only have to stand watch until daybreak. I doubt they'll try anything

once the sun is up and people are stirring.'

'Mrs Fowler said she'd be back in the morning.'

'Let's hope she brings her husband along,' Glen said. Mrs Fowler had said that she expected Sheriff Fowler to arrive tomorrow . . . or the next day. In a grim mood, Glen turned from the trembling blonde woman and stalked to the door.

The air outside was cold; Glen felt only the hot stirring of his blood as he trudged along the uneven path to the stable where his gray horse waited. Here and there along the main street men still roistered, having not a worry in the world. Dispiritedly, Glen envied them, having no worries but where their next drink was coming from.

Saddled up, Glen started from town riding directly toward the road to the J-Bar. He was confident that this was the direction Case would take, toward known country and, if necessary, to the refuge of the ranch proper. Wichita was

unlikely to charge into a manned camp. If Case had few friends at the ranch, still he had allies there.

Glen believed that Case would have a large lead on Wichita by now. Wichita had recklessly thrown himself on Case's trail. Glen, who had been forced on occasion to use such tactics himself, figured that Ben Case would have been clever enough to have circled back into town, lose his tracks among the myriad others along the streets, and then make his dash for the J-Bar. What Earl and Charles Buchanan had decided to do was anyone's guess. Possibly they too had ridden toward the J-Bar. It was just as likely that they had decided to fold their cards and get out of Big Springs before charges could be brought against them. It was an even bet. Earl, especially, valued that fifty thousand dollars above all else.

Glen wondered: if J. Pierce Buchanan could have foreseen what that missing money would cause, would he have written his last testament differently?

Certainly. Would it have made any difference in the long run? With the greedy men pursuing whatever they could profit from the old man's death, probably not.

By the faint silver light cast by the descending crescent moon, Glen reined in and swung down to look more closely at the pattern of tracks struck into the bare earth of the road to J-Bar Ranch. His gray horse, rested and eager to run now, tossed its head impatiently.

Glen could easily read his own horse's tracks and those of Amanda's sorrel travelling in the opposite direction, but he was unfamiliar with those of the animals the Buchanan brothers, Ben Case or Wichita and Toby rode. One thing was certain, however; four or five horses had passed this way and not long ago. It could have been any of a number of horsemen the way the area was being thronged, but Glen took the tracks as signs that his assumption was correct. They were heading for the J-Bar.

Glen heeled his horse forward, leaving the trail to pass over the south range. The herd assigned to the unlucky Fain brothers was drowsing at this late hour, appearing like a dark, nearly motionless mass. There was no sign of the Fains.

Glen reined in the gray horse and sat in the stillness, surveying the land. The J-Bar house was roughly a mile ahead in a direct line to the north. He remained certain that it would be Ben Case's destination and that Wichita would be on his trail, probably attempting to cut the foreman off before he could reach home and aid.

Case would be received without comment from the remaining hands, likely welcomed by Nora. If Case had managed to rejoin the Buchanan brothers, and the three of them, the ranch foreman and the heirs of J. Pierce together — could tell a convincing story, even Glen Strange might have a difficult time taking them. The remaining hands would fight for the brand.

Amanda was not here to vouch for his story, and to other ears it might not sound so believable.

Gloomily, but more determined than ever, Glen heeled his horse forward, aiming toward the low, pine-stippled hills ahead. Climbing slowly among the trees he soon found himself in deep shadows. The moon fell ever lower, the ranks of pines rose and the shoulders of the surrounding hills lifted higher against the blue-black star-cluttered sky.

Had it not been for his horse he might have ridden past the man without seeing him. The gray horse pricked its ears and flared its nostrils, blowing through them as it caught the scent of another pony and Glen had a glimpse of the man standing beside the huge pine tree, rifle positioned at his shoulder, sights fixed on him.

10

'Reverse your tracks, stranger, or I'll cut you down!' the familiar voice commanded.

'Wichita? It's Glen Strange!'

'Strange?' The rifleman lowered his weapon and eased out from beside the tree's trunk to face Glen, the moonlight showing his face clearly, illuminating the triumph written there. 'I've caught the bastard,' Wichita said proudly. 'Maybe you want to watch me talk to him.'

Glen didn't ask who Wichita meant. His only interest lay with Ben Case and what he felt the foreman owed him. There was little choice. Glen needed to know what was happening here and he did not think Wichita was going to just let him ride away even if he wished to. He swung down, carefully, from his horse's back and led the gray a dozen

yards into the forest, following Wichita.

In a small clearing, Ben Case sat cross-legged on the ground, his shirt torn, his hair in his eyes. Toby sat on a fallen tree to one side, his own rifle fixed on Case. The one-eared man appeared haggard, pain-ridden. His left leg showed the deep maroon stains of blood leaking from the gunshot wound he had suffered in Big Springs. It was a wonder the little man had made it this far. Case lifted bleary, angry eyes toward Glen and muttered something unintelligible.

'He's glad to see you,' Wichita said with a grin. 'Of course, he'd rather see you dead, wouldn't you, Carmody?'

Ben Case growled again. Wichita explained to Glen: 'Ben Carmody's his real name. The one he was using seven years ago, anyway. Isn't that right, Ben?' Ben Case or Carmody or whatever was in no mood for games.

'Is he hurt?' Glen Strange asked.

'Not as hurt as he's going to be,' Wichita vowed. 'His horse shied when

we burst upon him. It bucked and side-stepped, knocked Ben's head against a branch. We just had to pick him up and drag him back here for our talk.'

'There's nothing to talk about,' Case said, his anger gathering.

'Oh, there's a lot to talk about,' Wichita insisted. He crouched down, using his Winchester as a support. He tipped back his hat and went on, 'Like when, how, you're going to cough up what you owe me.'

'I don't have any money,' Ben Case said. Wichita rose, slugged him in the mouth and hovered over him as Case, reeling from the punch, spat blood. 'It's true,' he said painfully.

'I'll take a piece of this land then,' Wichita offered in a reasonable voice.

'It's not mine to offer,' Ben said. 'Tell him, Strange!'

Glen remained silent, gauging the situation, the probable result of this showdown, liking none of what he saw coming. Wichita was again in a crouch. Toby's attention seemed to be wandering. The

one-eared man had lost a lot of blood. He sat weaving back and forth on the fallen log.

Wichita went at Ben Case again. 'You wrote me, Ben. Told me that you were ram-rodding the J-Bar for an old man, nearly ninety years old. He was bound to go soon, you said, and the ranch would be yours.'

'He hung on for longer than I expected,' Ben said in a near-whisper.

'So you took care of that, didn't you?' Glen Strange shouted, no longer able to contain himself. Ben's eyes flashed.

'Yes, I did! He wouldn't tell me where he'd stashed the fifty thousand. I got damned mad. I shot him down! Are you satisfied now, Strange! I killed J. Pierce Buchanan. And it profited me nothing,' he added as if that had only now occurred to him.

'But you got the ranch,' Wichita suggested, 'or at least a part of it. He must have given you a part of the J-Bar.' His voice had become needful. He waited for the answer, mouth

slightly open, eyes anxious.

Ben Case looked as if Wichita had just demanded that he pull the drop lever on his own scaffold now that the noose had been fixed around his neck. 'Tell me!' Wichita demanded, rising to his feet again and Ben Case gave the only answer he could — the truth.

'I always thought I was going to come into some money, or at least a part of the J-Bar,' Case said, his voice as hollow as his eyes now, 'that was what J. Pierce told me. 'You won't have to worry about getting along after I'm gone, Ben,' he said. Those were his exact words. I didn't know that all he meant was that I'd still have my stinking job!'

'Which is more than I've got!' Wichita spat back furiously. 'Seven years sitting in a cell the size of a shoebox, roasting in the summer, freezing to the bone in the winter all because you were someone I once admired, someone I thought I could always count on. Damn you, Ben Carmody! Damn your eyes!'

Then he killed Ben Case.

Wichita made no pronouncement, uttered no curse or threat. He simply shouldered his rifle and shot the man. It was like watching a mad dog be put down, Glen Strange thought. He flinched as the shot was suddenly fired. Toby did not so much as blink when the sound of the shot roared in the clearing and gunsmoke curled up into the pines and was dissipated by the breeze.

The little man just said weakly, 'Wichita, I've got to get to a doctor or die.'

Wichita didn't respond. Instead he turned his dark eyes on Glen Strange and asked, 'Now what can I do?' as if it were something they had planned together all along.

'Head out of the country, I'd say. Before someone gets ideas about hanging you.'

'You! Would you turn me in, Strange?'

Glen had to shake his head. *No*. No, he thought, he wouldn't do that.

Wichita had saved him from having to use a bullet on Case himself.

'How can I ride out?' Wichita asked. 'I have a lot invested in this. Seven years is a long time, Strange. Riding all this way . . . have nothing.'

'There's nothing to have,' Glen said quietly to Wichita, who now faced him with hostile eyes as if Glen were partly to blame for his troubles.

'There's still the fifty thousand,' Wichita said, scratching his chin idly even as his eyes hardened and remained fixed on Glen Strange.

'No one knows where it is.'

'That lawyer does.'

'Case beat him nearly to death,' Glen said. 'The doctor says he'll be lucky if he survives.'

'No matter. The court or somebody will take over whatever business he leaves unsettled. The Buchanan brothers still stand to inherit the money.'

'If they can keep themselves out of jail,' Glen answered.

His words didn't seem to penetrate.

Wichita began slowly pacing in the darkness. To one side Toby simply sat sagged to one side. His eyes were open but contained little spark of feeling or concern. The one-eared Toby was another man not long for it, Glen thought.

'If we were to go back there tonight . . . ' Wichita's rifle suddenly came up again, his sights leveled on Glen's chest. 'Suppose you unbuckle that gun, Strange. That's exactly what we are going to do. Find the Buchanans and go back to the lawyer's office tonight! No one will expect it. All I've done,' he said, nodding at the crumpled body of Ben Case, 'is eliminate the middleman.'

'You'll never get in the office,' Glen said. As he spoke, he unbuckled his gunbelt with his left hand. He would have stood no chance against the two armed men watching his motions. Alive, he had a chance to stop this madness, dead he had none. His gunbelt dropped to the ground and

Wichita had him step away as he scooped it up.

'I don't particularly want to kill you, Strange. All I want you to do is help us out a little with this problem. What do you care about the gold? None of it will come to you anyway, will it?'

'No,' Glen admitted, 'but I can't see where I can help you either.'

'You can't?' Wichita's smile was ugly. 'That lawyer — I don't suppose he's alone in his office, is he?'

'No, he isn't. There's a very nervous lady there with a Colt .44 ready to shoot down anyone who tries to get in.'

Wichita's smile broadened; his eyes grew more cunning. 'Anyone but you,' he said. 'She wouldn't shoot you. That's where you can help me, Strange. The way you came to that lady's rescue, well, there's something between you two. If you're the first one through the door there won't be any shooting. Which is the best thing for everyone concerned, isn't it?'

'It won't work,' Glen repeated. 'The lawyer — '

'Who's to say he hasn't recovered by now! So what if he got pistol-whipped. We've both seen many a man survive something worse. No, he might be all right now, smiling at his good fortune. He won't be smiling when we go back there.'

'The law — '

'There is no law in Big Springs, and we both know it,' Wichita answered with contempt. 'Quit making excuses.'

'I'm not making excuses,' Glen insisted, spreading his hands, asking for belief. 'You don't even know where the Buchanan brothers are.'

'Maybe I don't need them at all,' Wichita countered.

'Not if you're good at safe-cracking, I don't suppose.'

'I'll play it any way it comes, Strange. One thing I will not do is leave without getting what I've come here for.' There was savage determination in the man's voice, in his eyes which glittered in the

feeble light of the stars and dying moon. 'Toby! Grab our ponies. We're riding.'

Toby rose stiffly to his feet, nodded at Wichita and then pitched forward on his face to lie unmoving against the pine needle strewn earth. The sustaining blood had finally leaked from his body. He was as dead as his motionless companion in the clearing, Ben Case.

Wichita's mouth tightened, but he only said. 'Come along, Strange. We've got another long ride ahead of us before this night is over.'

* * *

The moon was a dead memory, the night inky and cold as the two men approached Big Springs again from the south side of the town. On the streets, too, all seemed silent. The roisterers had drunk themselves to sleep, it seemed. Few lights burned across the rambling town. Nearing the hay barn again, they spotted the dark form of a

horse standing three-legged at rest outside the large front doors. A man stood nearby, preparing to mount.

'Well, would you look there,' Wichita said exultantly. 'Tell me that's not an old friend of ours!'

The tall, lean figure of the man in the narrow-crowned hat was unmistakable even at this distance and in the heavy darkness that had settled. It was Earl Buchanan, his movements uncertain, apparently undecided in his intentions. His head came up lethargically as Glen, followed by Wichita who carried his rifle across his saddlebow approached from the shadows.

'We came back,' Wichita said by way of greeting. Earl Buchanan's hawkish features tightened.

'So I see,' the Southerner drawled.

'You look like you're getting ready to pull out,' Wichita said. His horse shifted its feet under him, but he kept his rifle pointed in the general direction of both Glen and Buchanan.

'I can't see that it's any of your

business what I do,' Buchanan answered icily.

'You can't? It's simple. Ben Case has handed over his share of the money to me.'

'You're mad! Case would never — '

'I didn't say he handed it over voluntarily,' Wichita said in a tone which made his meaning clear. Slowly, Earl Buchanan turned that over in his mind. Wichita persisted: 'Why were you tied up with him anyway?'

'Frankly, I didn't feel that my brother and I were up to . . . what needed to be done. This man,' he nodded at Glen Strange, 'was on my sister's side and Case was supposed to be good with a gun. I thought we needed him.'

'Well, you can see now that Strange isn't a force to be reckoned with anymore. Case is gone, and let me tell you that I'm a better man with a Colt revolver than he ever was.'

Far across town a cock crowed and, glancing eastward, Glen saw the faintest gray glow in the sky. Wichita now

swung down from his horse, gesturing for Glen to do the same. The man continued to keep his rifle's muzzle trained on Glen.

'Did you hear that rooster, Buchanan?' Wichita said. 'We've got to make our move now, before the whole town's up and about. I don't know what deal you had with Case, but all I want is a split of the cash. You know where it is, don't you?'

Buchanan answered, almost wearily, 'We think it's still stashed in the safe in the lawyer's office. We couldn't get the combination to it out of Dumont because Case knocked his head in. As far as sharing the money . . . ' he told Wichita reluctantly, 'I'll go along with your proposition. What other choice do I have but to leave empty handed?'

'Good. What happened to your brother?'

'I'm afraid poor Charles wasn't up to the job,' Earl said with a lopsided smile. 'He's gone to the railroad depot to buy a ticket on the first train east.'

'Then you're not losing anything, are you?' Wichita said. 'You were going to have to split fifty-fifty with your brother, weren't you? Well, I'll take the same split.'

'Magnanimous of you,' Earl Buchanan muttered.

'Don't get snooty with me. I'm your only chance, and you know it. You hadn't an idea on how to handle this on your own. You're not thinking clearly. I see it this way. It's your money we're talking about after all. If we crash in to the lawyer's office and take it, well, they might call that coercion or recovery by force, whatever words the law might use, but it's not a robbery, you see? Not like it would be if I did it myself. With you along, well, I'm just helping you collect what's rightfully yours.'

'But how can we breach the door?' Buchanan wondered. 'There must be someone with Dumont. An armed someone, one assumes.'

'Only your sister,' Wichita said.

'She'd shoot me quicker than anyone

else!' Buchanan laughed humorlessly.

'And me,' Wichita said. Slyly he pointed out, 'But we've got our man, Strange here, to get us through the door. She damn sure won't shoot at him.'

'No,' Buchanan said, his expression slowly brightening as he studied Glen Strange. 'No, she wouldn't at that, would she? All right, let's have at it.'

'I don't think I care to help you,' Glen said evenly and both of the others shifted hostile eyes toward him.

'But you will,' Wichita replied, speaking between his teeth.

'Will I?'

'Yes, you will, and I'll tell you why. If you refuse, you die here. That means we'll have to break the lawyer's door down and there's sure to be shooting then. The girl is going to be the first one to catch lead. If she starts shooting at me, I won't have much choice, Strange. Think that over and tell me again that you don't care to help us.'

Glen did consider his options. He

had no reason to doubt Wichita's words. If all that stood between the outlaw and the fortune he felt he was owed was Amanda, yes, he would shoot her down. There was no choice but to play it their way. He cared nothing about the money. Let them have it. As Wichita had pointed out, it belonged to the Buchanan brothers anyway.

Amanda must not be harmed because of it. Ben Case was now out of the picture, none of the others had anything to gain by her death. Why would they harm her if he did as they requested? There was no choice. He nodded to Wichita.

'Let's have at it,' Glen said, glancing at the sky, 'before it gets any lighter.'

* * *

Amanda heard the soft sounds of approaching boots in the alley beyond the front door to Craig Dumont's office even through the veils of drowsiness surrounding her. She had been up most

208

of the night, expecting them to come, waiting for this moment. Now they had returned. She glanced toward the lawyer who still lay, arms folded across his chest, on the leather couch. He was as still as death, and several times during the long vigil Amanda had gone to him to check on his breathing. He was drawing in and expelling air, if shallowly. His body had been viciously shocked and it was slow to recover. Now and then Dumont had muttered a few words, but none that made any sense to Amanda.

The bootsteps halted before the door. Amanda drew back the curved hammer of the big Colt revolver with both thumbs. She had indicated to Glen that she knew how to use the weapon. That was true, but only after a fashion. Pistols were hardly unknown in Ohio, but she felt no confidence in her ability to hit what she was aiming at unless it was very close, and knew that she would not be quick to ready a second shot if one proved necessary.

She stood with the heavy pistol dangling from both hands, staring at the plank door to the office, hoping, praying that she had been wrong in her assumption. Perhaps she had heard only some passing stranger, a merchant making his way to his shop.

The thudding of a fist against the door rattled it in its frame and sent a spastic icy shiver down her spine. The pistol lifted slowly and her small finger tightened around the trigger. Gray light had begun to pale the high eastern window of the office.

The fist thudded against the door again.

11

'Who is it?' Amanda called, trying unsuccessfully to instill force in her voice.

'Me, Amanda,' the voice from beyond the door called. 'Glen Strange!'

'Glen?' She started that way, lowering the pistol and then halted, remembering. She had heard more than one set of boots. 'Who's with you?'

'Who's . . . ? A friend of mine. His name is Wichita. Let us in.' Glen's voice sounded edgy. Something was wrong. *Wichita?* Wasn't that the name of the man who had sent the obscure message that Glen had delivered to Ben Case, the one that had infuriated the ranch foreman?

Amanda hesitated, took half a step, lowered the pistol and took another half step, reaching down for the door latch. No sooner had the iron bar slid free

than they burst through the doorway. Glen, in front, was propelled roughly against Amanda and she dropped the gun which slid away across the floor. She was forced to cling to Glen to keep her balance. As they stood entangled, Wichita brushed past them into the room, followed by Earl. Amanda opened her mouth in a soundless complaint. Her eyes went wide with fear.

'There he is!' Earl said, striding to the leather couch where the lawyer lay, eyes closed, unmoving.

'He looks like he's dead,' Wichita said.

'He's only sleeping,' Earl Buchanan said frantically, 'or faking it.' He shook Dumont's shoulder roughly. 'Come on, you, wake up!'

'Leave him alone!' Amanda said. 'Haven't you done enough to him?'

'It was Case that did it,' Earl protested feebly.

'It was you who brought him here! The man's at death's door, can't you see that?'

'Looks like it,' Wichita said, casually raising one of Dumont's eyelids with his thumb. He turned on Earl Buchanan. 'Now what do you suggest?'

'What is there to suggest!' Earl said, more angry than ever. 'Sit him up! Slap him a couple of times. He'll come around. He's bound to.'

'Don't touch that man,' a quiet voice from the doorway said, and they turned to see a broad-shouldered man with a flowing white mustache standing there, pistol in hand. Sunlight gleamed on the badge pinned to his leather vest. 'The name's Fowler, and you all have a lot of explaining to do.'

Wichita wasn't in the mood for explanations; he was in the mood for fighting. The pistol in his hand slicked smoothly from his holster with the practiced motion of a gunman, and he turned the Colt on Sheriff Fowler. Both men fired at once. Wichita's hasty shot missed, splintering the doorframe beside Fowler's head. The sheriff's aim was truer. Wichita clutched his chest

and staggered backward, falling to the floor to lie still against the planks.

Earl Buchanan had been temporarily frozen with surprise. He was no gunfighter, but he was a desperate man. Feeling cornered, he had unwisely drawn his own weapon, but astonishingly he turned the muzzle not toward the sheriff, but toward Amanda.

As Wichita made his move, Glen Strange had already been diving for the Colt revolver that Amanda had dropped. Now, as the sheriff watched Wichita slam back against the floor to die, and Earl made ready to fire his weapon, Glen triggered off his pistol, firing from one knee. The bullet caught Earl Buchanan in the throat and he threw his hands up wildly, a cry of pain strangled by the sudden flow of blood there. Glen stepped to Amanda, put a supporting arm around her and faced the sheriff who was now holding his pistol aimed at Glen Strange.

'Drop it,' Fowler said and Glen opened his fingers, letting the weapon

clatter to the floor. 'Now let go of the girl and come over here and get dressed,' the sheriff said, displaying a pair of manacles.

'Him?' Amanda said in astonishment. 'Whatever for!'

'The charge is murder, miss,' the sheriff said evenly.

'Murder! But you saw what happened,' Amanda cried in disbelief. She still clung to Glen's arm.

'It's a murder charge, miss,' the sheriff answered. 'But not because of what happened here.' He nodded toward the unmoving figure of Earl Buchanan.

'Then what?' Glen began. A second man had appeared in the doorway beside the sheriff. Glen recognized him from the trail. He had a pouty little mouth, an unusually large lower body and vicious little eyes. He also wore a deputy sheriff's badge.

'That's him,' Abel Ward said to the sheriff. 'That's the man who murdered Po Hilgers.'

12

Glen Strange surveyed the spotless interior of the Big Springs jail from behind the iron bars of a cell. After fetching Dr Chambliss to tend to Craig Dumont, Mrs Fowler had rushed to the sheriff's office and now stood comforting Amanda and simultaneously casting a disapproving eye on her husband who, not so fastidious as she, leaned back in his chair, boots propped up on his newly polished desk. Fowler's hands were on his belly, and in his right hand he held a Colt revolver. His half-closed eyes appeared sleepy, but he was fully alert. He listened again to Deputy Ward's story, of finding Po Hilgers and another man dead on the road to the J-Bar, of recognizing Glen and Amanda as they rode away in the wagon.

'Yes, I was there!' Amanda nearly shouted, interrupting the deputy. 'And if you were there, you would have seen that this Po Hilgers and his confederate were trying to waylay and rob us on the trail. We were hauling my luggage back from the freight office,' she explained to Mrs Fowler.

'You lie,' Ward said unconvincingly.

'What I'd like to know is what Po Hilgers was doing out there instead of watching things in town,' Fowler said lazily.

'And you, Abel!' Mrs Fowler put in sharply. 'Why were you out on the J-Bar instead of tending to your duties?'

'I had reports of fortune hunters trespassing on J-Bar land,' Abel Ward muttered. 'I was obliged to check on things.'

From his cell Glen said, 'I saw you out on J-Bar two days earlier, north of the ranch. You were riding with two men. They looked like brothers. Both had hard-slanted cheekbones and prominent noses.'

'Sounds like the Wooden boys,' the sheriff said quietly. 'Were you out with them, Abel?'

'I took them on as special deputies.'

'What did they need that pick and shovel for?' Glen asked and he heard Abel Ward swear under his breath. The sheriff, even in apparent repose, frowned more deeply. He didn't like the way things were unraveling. It was one thing when Ward accused this Glen Strange of killing Po Hilgers, but the contradicting testimony of the lady owner of the J-Bar could not be taken lightly. And, obviously to Fowler — as his wife had complained to him that morning — his deputies had been among the gold seekers, not any impediment to them. Still, Fowler was generally a tolerant man. He decided that to resolve things, he would turn the J-Bar rider loose and allow Ward to keep his badge. At least for the time being.

At least, those were his intentions before the door to the sheriff's office

banged open and a trail-dusty, furious Austin Fain burst in. Startled, the sheriff let his feet drop to the floor, and he raised his pistol defensively.

'That man's a murderer!' Austin Fain said wildly. He was hatless and his fine blond hair hung in his eyes. His pointing finger was raised, his jaw now angrily set.

'Wait a minute, Austin — ' Glen began, but he and everyone else then realized that the pointing finger was not trained on Glen Strange, but on Deputy Ward.

'What's going on here, young man?' Fowler asked, coming to his feet. 'Calm down a little.'

Austin was so incensed that he was trembling. His finger remained pointed at Ward. His other hand rested dangerously close to his holstered pistol, something that did not go unnoticed by Sheriff Fowler.

'What are you talking about, son?' the sheriff asked. 'Tell me what's going on.'

'Me and my brothers were working the south range on the J-Bar. One of them was killed. I've kept my eyes open for Will's horse.' He looked at Glen. 'It was missing, you'll remember, Strange. I saw fresh tracks out on the north road this morning. Tracks I recognized. They were those I've seen for over two years now. The tracks of Will's pinto horse. If you'll look out at your hitch rail, Sheriff, you'll see a pinto pony wearing a J-Bar brand tied there.' He glared at Abel Ward.

'I ask you, Sheriff, who rode that pinto pony into town? Because whoever it was, that's the man who killed my brother. We were wrong, Strange, you and me. We thought no man could be low enough to kill Will that way just for a horse, but he did!'

'Just a minute!' Abel Ward screamed back. He backed away as the sheriff rounded his desk. Suddenly Ward's hand dropped toward his sidearm, but in backing the deputy had come up against the jail cell and

Glen Strange reached out through the bars, hooking his forearm around the deputy's throat, applying strangling pressure. Ward kicked and squirmed in Glen's grip, but it was no use.

The sheriff stepped to him and easily disarmed him. Unlocking the door with one hand, Fowler growled, 'Get out of there, Strange. There's only room enough for one man at a time,' and he shoved Ward face-forward into the cell.

* * *

'Three weeks,' Craig Dumont was explaining. He sat in his office chair, hands resting on his uncluttered desk. The swelling on his head had gone down, but he looked pale and still shaken by the pistol whipping. Now he lifted his eyes again to Amanda and Glen Strange. The front door to the office was open and a mild breeze drifted into the room. 'All J. Pierce asked of your brothers was that they remain here for three weeks. They

couldn't even wait that long,' he said dismally.

'He just wanted them to get to know the land, to love it as he did?' Glen asked.

'Yes,' Dumont answered. 'J. Pierce loved the high purple mountain peaks, the long valleys, the quick-running silver rills, the breadth and majesty of the land. He thought that once his three children came to know the land as he did they would never wish to leave it.'

'He was wrong,' Glen said. Amanda was holding his hand and she nodded silently.

'Yes, and it's too bad. But they had their own lives, their own interests. No man can expect everyone else to share his own interests, his own enthusiasms. If any of his grandchildren wished to stay, he would have been pleased. If any or all of you wished to go, well there was little he could do about it. His chief concern was that the three of you might not be able to decide upon how to divide the J-Bar.'

'He did not want the J-Bar divided anyway,' Glen commented.

'No. A man doesn't put fifty years of his life into something just to see it broken up. But J. Pierce thought he had found a way around that possibility.'

'The fifty thousand,' Amanda said.

'The fifty thousand,' Dumont agreed. He nodded toward his office safe. 'There never was any money in there, of course. There was never a hidden cache of gold on the J-Bar. No,' he shook his head. 'I don't know how that rumor got started. I suppose something like that always crops up when a fortune is involved.' He leaned back in his chair and smiled indulgently. 'Those people — the gold hunters — did not know how J. Pierce's mind worked, what he valued in this world.

'It was only land he cared for, only land he put his faith in. Not in banks or investments. Not even in gold, which may be lost or stolen.'

'And so he set out to make sure that all of his children were taken care of even if they could not agree among themselves what was to be done with the J-Bar,' Amanda suggested.

'Exactly,' the lawyer said. 'Those mysterious trips he took to Castle Rock and Cripple Creek were far from mysterious. J. Pierce was riding the land, shopping, and he purchased two smaller parcels, quite nice ranches with houses on them. One near Cripple Creek, one over by Castle Rock. These were to become the property of whichever of his children did not assume control of the J-Bar. He hoped, obviously, that the two would have come to love the country by then and wish to live on one of these two smaller parcels.

'Of course, being a realist, J. Pierce knew that his heirs might just choose to sell out and return east. In that case these smaller ranches could have been sold much more easily than the thirty-thousand acre J-Bar which J.

Pierce did not wish to have broken up in any case.'

'All of it was for nothing, then,' Amanda said, turning her eyes to Glen Strange. 'The scavengers crawling over our land, the killing, the death of my brother.'

'All of it,' Dumont said. 'Earl and Charles were each going to inherit one of the two distant ranches to manage or to sell as they chose. In return for waiting three weeks to come to know the country.'

Glen Strange was frowning. He spoke now: 'You know, Dumont, a few lives could have been saved if only you had spoken up earlier and explained about the legacy.'

Dumont looked dour, but somehow appeared offended as well. Lifting himself slightly in his chair, he answered stiffly, 'I am painfully aware of that, sir, but you must realize that I am an attorney and a man of my word. As difficult as it may have been, I was duty bound to adhere to the letter of my client's last wishes.'

★ ★ ★

'So what's going to happen now?' Bobby Trapp asked as he and Glen led their horses to the front porch of the big house on the J-Bar. Looking across the yard, Glen was pleased to see that Tiny and Calvin Traylor had finished rolling up the barbed wire that had surrounded Mae Buchanan's mausoleum.

'I don't know myself,' Glen replied. 'That's what Amanda wants to see us about.'

There she was, waiting on the porch in a white dress, a yellow ribbon in her blonde hair, hands clasped. They approached and tied their horses to the hitch rail.

'You've got it all sorted out?' Glen asked as he placed one boot on the lowest step and tilted back his hat.

'I think so,' Amanda said. 'After two more conferences with Craig Dumont.'

'How's he doing now?'

'Fine, it seems. Anyway, what I — we

— have come up with is this. Charles will have to be notified once more of his inheritance. I don't know how long it will take to contact him in Mississippi and for him to respond. Undoubtedly he will want to sell the ranch on Cripple Creek, and who knows how long that will take!'

'Quite a while, months anyway,' Glen guessed.

'That leaves the ranch at Castle Rock. There's a small house on it as well.' Amanda hesitated. 'I've offered it to Nora and she's accepted. She seemed shocked with the surprise of it, but as I told her, if you think about it, she was more of a grandchild to J. Pierce than any of the rest of us. She cooked and nursed him for years. She's welcome to it.' Amanda added: 'I think she's going to invite her mother to live with her.'

'The Paiute woman?' Bobby Trapp said in surprise.

'Yes. She's getting on in years, and the nomadic life of an Indian woman

227

can become grueling at her age.'

'Well, bless 'em both,' Bobby said. 'Does that mean that Tiny will — '

'I don't think Tiny wishes to rekindle whatever he shared with Nora's mother at this late stage of life. He'll be J-Bar's yard man forever,' Amanda said. 'Now, then!'

She continued after a pause for breath. 'There is the matter of caretaking the Cripple Creek ranch, the one that's been willed to Charles. It may be months, years, before anything's truly decided concerning the property. In the meantime we can't let it sit idle. I understand that the former owner is still on the land, anxious to leave. There is a small herd of cattle, the house. I need someone trustworthy to run the ranch for us while Charles decides what he will do.' Her eyes rested now on Bobby Trapp. 'How would you feel about being a ranch manager for a while, Bobby?'

'Me?' Bobby was honestly surprised. 'Well, sure. I mean . . . with my own

house and no boss standing over me? I'd be more than pleased, Miss Amanda.'

'That only leaves you, doesn't it, Glen?' Amanda asked, fixing those blue eyes on him. They now seemed to have the depth and the warmth of the blue flame at the base of a candle wick.

'I don't know what you mean,' Glen Strange answered.

'Well,' she said, 'you could go along with Bobby and help him get the Cripple Creek ranch going.'

'Is that what you want me to do?'

'It's up to you,' Amanda said. 'Of course, I do need someone to take Ben Case's place and run the J-Bar for me.'

'I guess I could take that job,' Glen agreed.

'That is, if you wanted to. You can have Ben's old room in the big house. If you like.'

'If you think that's the best arrangement.'

'It might be, if you want that,' Amanda said.

'I wouldn't mind, if that's what you really want,' Glen Strange said.

'It's entirely up to you, Glen. I want you to do what you want to.'

'I guess that would be all right with me — if you're sure that it's a good idea,' Glen was saying as Bobby Trapp walked to his horse and swung onto the saddle. It was a long ride to Cripple Creek and high time he was going.

Neither Amanda Buchanan nor Glen Strange turned to watch him as he drifted his pony away from the house, passing through the shadows of the old oak trees.

We do hope that you have enjoyed reading this large print book.

Did you know that all of our titles are available for purchase?

We publish a wide range of high quality large print books including:
Romances, Mysteries, Classics
General Fiction
Non Fiction and Westerns

Special interest titles available in large print are:
The Little Oxford Dictionary
Music Book, Song Book
Hymn Book, Service Book

Also available from us courtesy of Oxford University Press:
Young Readers' Dictionary
(large print edition)
Young Readers' Thesaurus
(large print edition)

For further information or a free brochure, please contact us at:
Ulverscroft Large Print Books Ltd.,
The Green, Bradgate Road, Anstey,
Leicester, LE7 7FU, England.
Tel: (00 44) **0116 236 4325**
Fax: (00 44) **0116 234 0205**

Other titles in the
Linford Western Library:

UNSIGNED AVENGER

John Davage

When Will Cord is shot dead for the brutal killing of Ali Toombs, Joe Hayes and his two sons know the real killer is still at large . . . Could it be Cole Sanderson — a newcomer to Consolation? Saloon girl Maggie Brown knows he's not who he says he is. Or could it be Lew Rosen, editor of the *Gazette*, who suspects the Hayes brothers? Fear and suspicion spread like a prairie fire — is anyone safe from accusation and violence?

FAITH AND A FAST GUN

Chap O'Keefe

Joshua Dillard, the ex-Pinkerton detective, on a sentimental journey to a mission graveyard in Texas, had ridden into trouble. Guns blazed around the headstones as he intervened to save a girl called Faith from the clutches of Lyte Grumman and his gunhawks. Grumman, a cattle baron, believed that a rigged poker game had lost him a thousand head of longhorns. Now he was intent on recouping his loss, whatever it took — and Joshua's Colt Peacemaker was hopelessly outnumbered . . .

GUNS OF PONDEROSA

Chuck Tyrell

When Nate Cahill and his gang take over the town of Ponderosa, sawmill magnate Fletcher Comstock sends for his friend Matt Stryker. However, Cahill is waiting for him. He gelds Stryker's fine Arabian stallion and beats him terribly. But Stryker will not give up. He pins on the marshal's badge, tames a rowdy town and gets rid of the ruthless Cahill gang. Now the guns of Ponderosa blaze and blood runs red in the Arizona high country.